+Catherine Colson-Sayers (CCS) Investigations

Book One : MISSING

BY

Susan Elle

For

Ursula Publishing UK

Missing
Text Copyright © 2013
by Susan Elle
Ursula Publishing UK
All Rights Reserved

This book is a work of fiction. Names and Characters are the product of the author's imagination and any resemblance to actual persons, living or dead, is entirely coincidental.

Cover Photograph
©mirceadfa /Dreamstime.com

ISBN   978-1-910753-11-8

Other Books by Susan Elle

The Sara Colson Trilogy
Sara's Child
Sara's Loss
Sara's Shame
All the above also available as audio books.

Catherine Colson-Sayers Investigations
(CCS Investigations)
Book 1 : Missing
Book 2 : The Chosen
Book 3 : Travis
Book 4 : Deleted
Book 5 : Mind Games (twice the length of previous
Books) due out end August 2015

Tempest
Broken

Love, Lies & Consequences Trilogy
Book One : Love
Book Two : Lies
Book Three : Consequences

Langdon Trilogy
Heart & Home
Heart of a Lion
Heart of Stone
http://www.susan-elle.com

Table of Contents

PROLOGUE

"Ok, mum, I'll be back at tea-time and I'll be bringing Josh home with me." Nat shrugs on a lightweight cardigan and hooks her shoulder bag in place.

"Don't forget your sunscreen, you know how badly you burn and the sun is fierce at the moment!" Natalie's mum comes out of the kitchen holding a bottle of sunscreen out in front of her.

Smiling at her daughter, Fiona Richerson counts her blessings. Unable to have any more children, she is very protective of Natalie and loves her deeply.

"Thanks mum."

Stepping out into the bright sunshine, Natalie gives Josh a wave. He waiting in the blue Venga that his mum and dad bought for his eighteenth birthday. Since then they have enjoyed lots of days out as both of them love walking in the countryside.

"Hi gorgeous," Josh leans over to kiss Nat as she climbs into the passenger seat.

"I'm really looking forward to this," Nat smiles radiantly at Josh. "Are we really driving to Derbyshire? The online photos do look beautiful."

"It won't take us long up the M1," Josh assures her. "And Matlock is worth the trip."

The radio is playing the latest pop tunes and they are both singing along. The mood is light, and right now their futures look as bright as the summer day.

"Has your mum let up about your applications to uni'?" Nat asks as Nora Jones sings the final notes of 'Come Away With Me'.

Josh grimaces, "Not really, they still prefer Oxford." Pulling up at the traffic lights he turns to Nat, "I can sort of understand it – it's where they met and they both did really well there."

Feeling her heart sink in to her boots, Nat bites down on her bottom lip. "Have you changed your mind?"

Covering her hand with his, Josh gives it a gentle shake. "Don't talk crazy – I can't wait to go to Eastbourne with you," he tells her, frowning at her for doubting him. "I love you, Nat – we'll have a great time sharing student accommodation — though not in halls, I don't think universities are that liberal minded yet."

They both laugh, each silently contemplating the next three years that they have planned to spend together studying...and loving each other without well-meaning parents forever looking over their shoulders.

What would they think if they told them that they were both still virgins? They'd been together since Josh and his family had moved to the area and he'd started at Nat's school.

That was five years ago — they'd been just thirteen, two shy teenagers who'd found a like friend and then the friendship had grown into so much more.

At eighteen, they were both applying to university. Nat's parents were happy for her to go to Eastbourne — it had exactly the course she wanted to study and their visit to the campus had been really positive.

It was just Josh's parents who were holding back, preferring their son to follow in their own footprints and gain the prestige of being educated at Oxford University.

Nothing seemed to get through. Even when Josh filled out his application to Eastbourne, which offered courses just as good as Oxford did, they still didn't relent.

'You can't live your life around Natalie,' his mother had told him only last night. 'Your whole future hangs on not only your grades, but the perception of you as a person. Oxford can only add quality to that perception, whereas Eastbourne...adds nothing at all.'

No, they hadn't let up, but he and Nat were determined to make up their own minds about their future. They had already decided that being apart for most of the next three years was not even a remote possibility.

It took a couple of hours to reach Matlock; they hadn't been in any rush and their lovely day just got better and better.

"Oh, Josh, this is so beautiful," Natalie gazes around her at the open expanses. Holding her arms out wide and her face up to the sun, she closes her eyes and turns in circles like a little girl.

After watching her carefree playfulness, Josh moves forward to catch Nat around the waist. "Come on, you'll get dizzy if you keep whirling like that and I want to reach that peak before lunch time," he grins, pointing all the way to the top of a nearby hill of considerable size.

"I love you, Joshua Turner," she laughs, as her head continues to whirl. "I can't wait for Eastbourne...and after that, we won't ever be apart again."

"Never," Josh holds a tender hand to her cheek and his eyes hold a promise that he is determined to keep.

"When we get married it will be for keeps." Lifting his hand to hold her long auburn hair out of her eyes, Josh leans in for a kiss. "I can't wait to make love to you – I must dream about you every night."

Nat looks a little worried. "But we made a promise," she frowns, her smile now hesitant, "to save ourselves until our wedding night – you haven't changed your mind have you?"

Taking her hand, Josh begins to lead her along the well-worn trail they're following. "I haven't changed my mind," he confirms. "But that doesn't mean a man can't dream, does it? Don't you ever imagine what it will be like – just to lay together and know that we're exactly where we belong, that loving each other physically is the last step to making us complete as a couple."

Blushing, Natalie nods and lets her long hair fall forward to hide her embarrassment. "Sometimes I wake up hot and aching, but I love that we're waiting for marriage. So many youngsters our age seem to think that sex is like smoking, just something you do to make you look more grown up and socially cool – I love that you want us to wait."

The sun is shining down and the sky is clear and blue; with their shared dreams in the forefront of their minds they ascend the challenging hill side trail hand in hand.

CHAPTER ONE

Looking up at the bedroom ceiling, Catherine smiles as Logan lays a hand on her swollen abdomen to feel their babies kick.

"You know, you're only twenty-six weeks along," Logan muses, watching as his sons cause their mum's stomach to protrude at odd angles, "I just can't imagine the size you'll be in another fourteen weeks."

"Oh great – I already feel like a beached whale and you're imagining me looking like a flaming elephant!" *Not that I care – amazingly, I love being pregnant. Well, now I do – it just creeped me out at first.*

"You're always beautiful to me," Logan grins up at her, knowing that Catherine isn't a vain woman and is enjoying her pregnancy now.

Her hand comes to lie besides Logan's on her stomach. "Our boys are in there," she frowns with amazement, "I don't think I'll really believe it until they're out. It just seems impossible."

"It is a miracle and no mistake," Logan agrees. Then he reaches up to kiss her soundly, tenderly. "I love you, Mrs Colson-Sayers," he tells her softly, "you've made me so happy – I can barely remember my life without you in it."

"Is that a good thing?" she asks, still looking for the catch in her perfect life – the punch-line that will come before the fall.

"It's a very good thing," Logan's smile broadens, then his eyes fly open wide as he feels the twins give enormous kicks.

"Christ almighty," Catherine laughs uncertainly, "I think Fred and George are already beating each other up in there – they'll be black and blue by the time they're born!"

"Have we settled on names yet?" he asks, his hand resuming its massage of her stomach with the oils that Caroline bought her. "I know you didn't like James or Jason, but you said you were considering Andrew, Michael and Adam."

"And Christopher," Catherine adds. Taking a huge breath in, she blows it out again slowly and pulls at her bottom lip. "Maybe we could try switching them around a bit – we'll need middle names too, I suppose?"

"We don't have to – what do you think of Andrew and Adam Sayers?" he asks thoughtfully.

A slow smile spreads over Catherine's face. *Andrew and Adam – it makes them more real to think of them with names. Like...Andrew will you stop hitting your brother – or, Adam stop throwing stones! I'm going to be a mum...me!*

"You look dreamy and happy – what's going on in that super-brain of yours?" Logan chuckles deep and low.

"I'm going to be a mum," she tells him like it's breaking news. "How the heck am I going to know what to do – they don't exactly come out with a manual in their little hands?"

"I have no idea how to be a dad either," Logan reminds her. "We'll just have to do what everyone else does, learn as we go along and hope for the best."

"At first, I thought it was scary just the thought of having something growing inside of me." Catherine strokes her stomach in wonder, "and then it was scary thinking about how I was going to get them out – I mean, you have to admit, you would not voluntarily try to squeeze something as large as a baby out through your backside, and it's the same thing if you look at it size wise."

Logan grimaces and looks up at Catherine. "That is some image you just put into my head – thanks for that."

"Well it's no worse than the reality I'll be facing in another fourteen weeks," she tells him. "It still scares the hell out of me, no matter how many times I watch the damned video."

They had watched the video that the midwife had given them together, when Catherine had been just twelve weeks pregnant and her stomach was only just starting to bloom. It had made them both cringe and gape and gasp, with regular cries of 'that just isn't possible' and 'I'll never be able to do that'.

"I'll be right there with you," Logan kisses her stomach then lies back down alongside her and pulls Catherine into his arms.

Giving his arm a sharp punch she says, "Too damned right you will – if I'm going to be in agony you're going to be right there to witness it. Then I can make you feel guilty after and you'll be willing to do anything to make up for it," she laughs and kisses his bare chest.

Stretching his arm down to cup her bottom, Logan pulls her more firmly against him. "I can make a start on that right now," he suggests with a sexy groan in her ear. "What would madam like me to do first – this, or this, or maybe this," he demonstrates, nibbling her ear and working his way down to her swollen breasts and proud nipples.

Oh boy! "Just keep trying things out for a while," she gasps as he takes her nipple between his lips, "and I'll let you know."

Her breasts have become extra sensitive during the pregnancy and Logan pays them particular attention.

Catherine shudders when his tongue does a rapid flick over their tightening tips then takes them between his lips in turn to suckle gently.

"I might get jealous when the boys arrive," leaning on his elbows Logan lifts his head to look at Catherine, his hands gently massaging her breasts. "These have always been exclusively mine; I'm not sure how I'll feel about sharing."

"Logan..." Catherine gives a shudder as his thumbs nonchalantly flick over her nipples, "...can we discuss the pros and cons of breastfeeding later, you're driving me crazy."

"I live to serve," he chuckles before diving under the quilt to suckle on another love bead that has her shuddering to her core in thirty seconds flat.

Mrs Baines serves them breakfast in the conservatory, the bright June sun shining through the windows to bathe them in the warmth of another lovely day.

"How are you this morning?" she asks Catherine, as she places a plate of scrambled eggs on toast in front of her.

"Never better, this pregnancy lark actually seems to suit me," she replies, sounding pleasantly surprised.

"Yes, you were lucky to escape the dreaded morning sickness," Mrs Baines nods and pours her a glass of fresh orange juice. "I hear Adrianne hasn't been so lucky, though Caroline seems to be coasting along just like you."

"That's because we're the same," Catherine states confidently. "I mean we actually came from the same egg and sperm, they just split off to make two babies – Adrianne is one on her own, though I wish she'd inherited whatever the damn gene is that stops Caroline and I from suffering the sickness that Adrianne does. If she loses much more weight she'll be all skin and bone and baby!"

"Hmm...it's a shame they had to come back early from their honeymoon," Logan observes, "but Robert said there was no point staying when Adrianne was obviously too unwell to enjoy it."

Catherine looks down at her plate and tries not to be jealous of her lovely sister. "Her mum has taken time off work to stay with her until it passes...that's nice," she adds wistfully.

A concerned glance passes between Mrs Baines and Logan that Catherine, thankfully, doesn't see. She's been getting broody; a large article in the local newspapers raked up all the gruesome details of her mother's murder in the wake of Charlie Edwards' recent trial and conviction.

The article detailed the fact that Catherine and Logan had been actively involved in bringing Charley Edwards to justice. It hadn't gone into how they had been involved, and Logan could only think that Inspector Harper, while giving them some credit for their hard work, had not elaborated further.

"We could drive over to see her after breakfast, if you like?" Logan offers, concerned that Catherine seems to have been avoiding Adrianne of late.

"That's ok, I spoke to her on the phone last night – she said her mum was fussing over her and the baby seems to be weathering it all ok," Catherine replies, cutting up her scrambled eggs on toast but not really eating any of it.

Reaching over to take her hand, Logan waits for Catherine to look at him, "The fact that her mum is with her, and yours can't be, shouldn't come between you." His brows are pulled together over concerned brown eyes, "You have a family now, Catherine – with family comes responsibility, to love, to care, to be there for each other when the going gets rough. I know Adrianne is concerned for you after that article appeared in the newspaper – don't you think she'd like the opportunity to make sure that you're ok?"

Still pushing her breakfast around her plate, Catherine considers. *I don't even know why it hurts so bad...it's not like I never had a mother...not like Caroline. I just wish she was here, I miss you so damned much, mum.*

"I don't want to make her sad, or worried, just because I'm no good at this family stuff," she tells him, finally putting her knife and fork down on her untouched breakfast. "I don't even understand what's wrong with me – sometimes I just cry for what seems like no reason at all, and then I find myself thinking of mum and wishing she was here to help me through all this. I just don't know, Logan. I don't know anything about this family stuff...about having sisters...or having my own children – I'll probably screw them up..."

"Enough!" Logan gives the hand he is holding a firm shake. "I won't sit here listening to you pull yourself to pieces." Lifting the hand he's holding to his lips, Logan looks determined. "I couldn't ask for a more loving, capable wife than you. What you give is instinctive...there is nothing calculated or contrived about your love – you give what you truly feel inside, and I guarantee, when you hold our boys in your arms," he tells her while smiling proudly down at her swollen belly, "you will love them and protect them just as instinctively."

Tears are building in Catherine's blue eyes and her bottom lip is caught between her teeth to stop it trembling. "You seem to have a lot of faith in me – I don't know where you get it from, but thanks anyway."

Pulling Catherine to her feet by the hand he is still holding, Logan moves in to wrap his arms around his woman. "You're mine. I know you better than you do, and I love that I get to see the real, honest to goodness loving, caring woman that you are." Laying his cheek on the top of her hair, his hands caress her back, "You can be as prickly and defensive as you like with others, but I know you're just a pussycat underneath those tiger's claws you use so effectively...but that's our secret. Ok?"

Catherine has to stand slightly side on to get as close to Logan as she likes, his smell alone calms her, his strength and love soothing all her insecurities...again. "I love you," she breathes into the familiar warmth of his broad chest, "but if you tell anyone that I'm a pussycat, I'll show you just how sharp these tiger's claws really are," and she playfully digs her nails into his firm bum.

With a deep chuckle, Logan gives Catherine another hug. "Now you're giving me other ideas and they don't include getting ready to visit Adrianne – behave yourself, or I'll ravish you right here and now!"

"Ok, ok," Catherine concedes, but not before giving his lovely rear end another good squeeze. "It's your own fault for being so damned...well I don't know what you'd call it, but my hands just seem to love your body," she smiles and frowns up at him, giving a 'I can't help it' shrug.

"And my body seems to love your hands," Logan grins down at her impish face then down to the growing bulge in his trousers, "but I'm not giving into them – go do what you need to do, we're going over to see Adrianne as soon as you're ready."

The drive is comfortable and pleasant, the countryside in full bloom and glorious in its many colours. England seems to be enjoying the best summer it has had in years.

"Can you believe this weather..." Catherine turns a happy smile to Logan, "...it's been like this for weeks now."

"It is amazing," he agrees, "though it might not be so pleasant for you expectant ladies as you progress."

Narrowing her eyes, Catherine turns in her seat to face Logan, "You seem to have a fixation on pregnant women and their increasing size. Are you going off me already?"

Giving a hearty laugh Logan pulls the Mercedes up in front of the mansion house where Adrianne and Robert live. "Did it seem like I was going off you this morning when I tasted those lovely round breasts?" he asks with a low, sexy growl. "Or when you came so hotly over my tongue..."

"Ok, ok!" She has grown hot and her breathing has shallowed and it has nothing to do with the heat of the day. "Jesus...we're outside my sister's house and you're putting embarrassing pictures in my head." Putting a hand to her hot cheeks she sighs heavily, "And they'll know. No doubt they'll think we've been canoodling in the car or something even worse!"

Logan unbuckles their seatbelts and pulls her in for a cuddle. "They will if we sit here much longer," and he kisses the tip of her nose.

"Oh great!" Catherine feels her cheeks grow even hotter as she spots Adrianne's mother at the open front door.

Lorna lifts concerned eyes to Catherine when she rounds the car to the house. "You look a little flushed, is this heat getting too much for you dear?"

With a quick 'I told you so' glare at Logan, Catherine allows herself to be ushered into the main lounge and over to a plush settee where Adrianne is waiting to greet her.

"Oh, Catherine," Adrianne throws her arms around her big sister's neck and promptly bursts into tears, "I've been so worried about you. All those horrid newspaper stories..."

Looking up at Logan in alarm, Catherine begins to stroke Adrianne's long black hair and just hopes her sister's sobs stop sometime soon. "Don't upset yourself on my account," she tells her, "you know I'm tough as old boots."

Pulling back, Adrianne uses a tissue to wipe her eyes and nose, and then gives Catherine a tremulous smile, "I know that's what you want people to think, but I know better. We're sisters," she says simply, at Catherine's frown.

"Have you two been talking about me?" she asks, looking from Adrianne to Logan, who is now smiling with a self-satisfied look of 'I told you so' on his too handsome face. "Hmm!"

"It makes me feel so wretched to know you went through all of that on your own," Adrianne sniffs into her tissue. "And I had such a loving home," and looks up at Lorna who is standing nearby, "it just doesn't seem fair."

But Catherine shakes her head firmly, "I'm glad you and Caroline were spared that – I wouldn't wish that nightmare on my worst enemy." Then, lifting Adrianne's chin, Catherine gives her a rueful smile, "You're not the only one who's had problems with the waterworks," and turns a smile on Logan. "I'm told it's got something to do with hormones – though how a man knows anything about a woman's hormones beats me."

Lorna gives a small chuckle, "It so happens that Logan is right on this account. Most pregnant women go through spates of crying for what seems like no reason at all – it doesn't do them any harm, for the most part."

"Well, I don't remember hearing Caroline say she's having any problems with hormones or crying jags," Catherine considers with a vague frown.

"Oh yes, yes she has," Adrianne pipes up suddenly. "We went for a walk together in the park last week – you remember, I telephoned you to come with us but you said you were busy with something," Adrianne reminds her and Catherine feels her cheeks heat up again. "Well, we came across a little girl pushing the cutest pink pram with a dolly inside and Caroline went to pieces – just started blubbering about how cute she looked and how she couldn't wait to see her own girls pushing their little prams in the park."

"Jesus!" Catherine's eyes go wide and a look of relief passes over her face before she can hide it from Logan who raises an eyebrow at her. "Well...I...I'm sure you managed to calm her down...or cheer her up...or whatever the hell you do for someone whose crying buckets." *Bloody hell! How am I supposed to know what you do for crying females – sisters or not, it's all new to me!*

Suddenly, Adrianne's arms are wrapped around Catherine's neck again and she can feel her younger sister begin to shudder with tears again. "I'm so glad you came – I love you, Catherine!"

Giving her sister a momentary squeeze, Catherine pulls back and raises an eyebrow at her, "If you're so damned pleased to see me why are you crying again?"

Then Adrianne blinks rapidly, and begins to laugh, "I have no idea, I blubber whether I'm happy or sad – the waterworks just spring a leak at the oddest moments."

Hmm, thank god mine are not that bad, I'd never be able to leave the house!

CHAPTER TWO

"You liked her!" Logan points his fork at Catherine.

"Lorna's ok," Catherine concedes reluctantly. "The best part is, she's a doctor so Adrianne is in good hands."

Catherine bends her head low over their evening meal. They had spent the rest of the morning with Adrianne and had even stayed for a light lunch. It had taken a while, but Catherine had warmed to Lorna when she saw how well she cared for her baby sister.

"You don't need to hide your feelings from me, Catherine," Logan tells her, watching the way Catherine is avoiding his gaze. "Love is new to you, and what you feel for your sister is a mixture of love, protectiveness and jealously – a confusing mixture for most of us."

"Yeah, well...she's the baby," Catherine says, as if that explains it all. "And I suppose...shit...Lorna's not so bad."

Then, with a wide-eyed gasp, she looks over at Logan then down at her stomach and claps her hands over each side like she's covering a child's ears, "Now see what you made me do...I just swore in front of the children!"

Logan's head is thrown back and the deepest, loudest laughter erupts from him. Even Mrs Baines is drawn back into the conservatory to see what all the sudden hilarity is about.

"Well now, you sound happy," Mrs Baines observes, wiping her hands on a towel as she stands smiling in the doorway. But when she looks over at Catherine the smile falters, "Are you alright, Catherine?"

She is frowning over at Logan, her hands still clasped on either side of her belly. "The lunatic thinks it funny to make me swear in front of the children," she states, and turns her furrowed brow on Mrs Baines who has to bite discretely down on her bottom lip to stop herself from joining in with Logan's laughter.

Taking a steadying breath, Mrs Baines smiles reassuringly at Catherine, "Were they kicking at the time — did you feel them moving?" At Catherine's slow shake of her head, Mrs Baines lets her smile become a grin. "Then you're off the hook, they're sleeping and won't have heard a thing."

Looking doubtfully down at her stomach, Catherine considers then glares over at Logan, "You moron! You know it's hard for me to kick the habit of a lifetime..." Her brows begin to iron out, her blue eyes softening as she takes in the sight of her beautiful husband. *Damn it...he looks so happy, and he really seems to love me – go figure!*

Suddenly all heads turn to look in the direction of the front door, then back to look at each other.

"Are we expecting visitors?" Logan asks, the doorbell having been rung by an unknown someone.

Mrs Baines shakes her head, "Not as far as I know."

"Me either," Catherine tells him, her frown back in situ.

Getting up from his chair, Logan tells them, "I'll go – you finish your dinner..." and waves a hand at Catherine as he passes on the other side of the table, "...you haven't eaten nearly enough today."

Walking towards the solid wood door, Logan is turning possibilities over in his mind. If it's Ben with more work for Catherine he can take a hike – she needs her rest and isn't sleeping well at all just now.

Reaching for the door, he opens it and finds himself looking down at a frail looking woman, though she isn't lean of body.

"Are you alright...?" he asks with concern. "May I help you...?"

Her bottom lip trembles and Logan looks past her to see if there is anyone with her, but sees only the woman looking close to tears. "I need to speak with Catherine Colson," she begins, trying to put some strength into her tremulous voice. "They told me in the town that she lives here."

Logan steps back and waves the woman in, then ushers her into the lounge and to a settee. Once he has her seated, Logan takes a nearby armchair and watches as the woman takes some papers from her small handbag.

"I came because of this," and she hands him an article she has cut out of a newspaper. "Is it true what they say...did she find her mother's murderer after all these years?"

No sign of the laughter is left in Logan's eyes as he looks down at the press cutting and then back at the woman. He nods and sighs heavily, "It is – but why does that bring you here?"

Taking out more papers she shuffles through them then hands a photograph to Logan. "That's my daughter, Natalie, and her boyfriend, Joshua – they've been missing for a week now and the police don't seem to have any idea what's happened to them."

The woman's hands are clutching her handbag on her knee, but still her hands tremble. "And you think Catherine might be able to help find them?" he asks tentatively. He watches as the woman nods and feels his heart sink.

If Catherine gets into this she won't rest until they're found, and she isn't resting nearly enough as it is. But they are missing... Holding the photograph out to the stranger in his lounge, Logan watches her put everything neatly away. *I can't just turn her away! Maybe I can...*

But any ideas he may have had were obliterated as Catherine enters the room. "May I see the photo?" Crossing the room, she takes a seat beside the woman who retrieves the photo from her bag and hands it to Catherine. "They look happy," she states with a concerned smile. "Are you sure they didn't just run off together?"

"That's what the police think – I know it," the woman takes out a tissue and dabs at her sunken eyes. "But they don't know my Natalie, and Joshua is a good boy, they would never do that. Never!"

Nodding, Catherine reaches out to take the woman's trembling hand. "What's your name...?" she asks quietly, "...and where do you live?"

"I'm Fiona Richerson, and we live in Upper Stanton, but that's not where they disappeared from," she tells them. "They both love walking — they often go off to different parts of the countryside for the day, and they're both members of a rambling society." She stops, closes her eyes and her exhaustion seems bone deep. "They drove to Matlock, in Derbyshire — now that Joshua has the car his parents bought him for his eighteenth birthday, they take off a lot."

Logan gets to his feet and puts a gentle hand on the woman's shoulder. "I'm just going to get us some tea," he tells her, "or coffee, if you would prefer?"

Giving a grateful smile up at him, Fiona says, "A strong cup of tea would be most welcome — thank you."

"Has anything like this ever happened before?" Catherine probes gently.

"Never!" Fiona's voice is resolute. "Natalie has never given me a minute's worry — she calls if she's going to be late and lets me know if she isn't going to be where she said." Fiona gives a mirthless laugh, "I said Natalie has never given me a minute's worry — well, that is not quite correct," Fiona states, her brows drawn together over a troubling memory. "When she was fourteen, Natalie told me she was going to study with her friend, Katy, and stay overnight."

"But she didn't?" Catherine asks when Fiona falls silent.

"No...no she didn't," Fiona seems to pull herself back from a particularly difficult memory. "At least...she did, but then another friend invited them both over for a group study session and they stayed the night there."

Her head shakes in wonder. "That was the night Colin took ill, I telephoned the number Natalie had given me but she wasn't there – I was frantic." Her lovely face pulls into a winsome smile, "She's never done anything like it again – it frightened her as much as me. 'What if it had been serious', she kept saying. And I had to agree, if Colin's acute indigestion had turned out to be the heart attack we'd both feared it was, I might not have found her in time for her to see her dad before...before...well..." she tails off, not wanting to finish the unhappy thought.

"But since then," Catherine asks, "she's always let you know where she is or if her plans have changed?"

"Always!" Fiona is adamant. "Oh, I know what the police think; I saw the sceptical look they gave each other when they didn't think I would notice. But Natalie is a good girl, she would never worry me like this...especially after what happened before!"

"Ok," Catherine murmurs, trying to pull her thoughts into order, "so we know that wherever she is, Natalie didn't go willingly."

A sob tears from Fiona, her hand flying up to cover her mouth, "You believe me," she tells Catherine, after swallowing down the tears that are threatening to fall. "You really believe they're missing!" Closing her eyes, Fiona pulls herself in and then looks at Catherine with something akin to relief. "No one will take me seriously, you're the first person to really listen and not just pay lip-service to what others have seen as a doting and deluded mother."

Cautiously, Catherine reassures the barely in control mother that she has only just met. "I do believe you, but I'm not sure what I can do to help?"

Taking a tissue from her handbag, Fiona dries away the threat of tears and sits with a straightened spine. "You've already done my heart good just by believing that they are both missing – now there are at least three people in this world who know that to be a fact." Lifting her chin, as if readying herself to take a hard knock, Fiona gives Catherine a determined look. "I'll understand if you want no more to do with this," she tells her, her eyes lowering to look at Catherine's swollen belly, "I had no idea that you were pregnant – but I'm desperate enough to ask for your help anyway."

Catherine gets up just as Logan returns with a tea tray and a plate of biscuits. She paces the lounge, her thoughts going round in circles as she tries to decide what to do. *How can I just send her away...just get on with my own comfortable life while those kids suffer God knows what?* She glances over at Fiona, watches as her lovely husband fusses over the woman. *But what exactly does she expect from me – the safe deliverance of her daughter...? I can't promise that!*

With some trepidation, Catherine retakes her seat and picks up the tea Logan has poured for her. "I'm not promising anything more than that I will give your request some serious consideration," she begins tentatively. "This would be a lot to take on, especially now," Catherine's free hand lovingly strokes her belly, "my boys will always come first."

"Boys...you're having twins...?" Fiona smiles in wonder.

"Yes, I'm one myself and I'm looking forward to meeting our sons in about fourteen weeks' time," Catherine beams over at Logan, who returns her smile with an ocean of love.

"I can't deny, I would be worried about the effect all this might have on Catherine and the boys if she were to take this on," Logan tells Fiona honestly. "I saw what it did to Catherine when she searched for her mother's murderer — she was successful, but it came at a heavy price."

Fiona nods her head, her expression having gone forlorn. "I see. I see," she mumbles softly.

But Catherine can't bear the other woman's look of abject defeat. "Look, I'm not saying no...at least, not altogether," she qualifies when Logan frowns. "Just give me some time to think this over, get some idea of what I can and can't do." Looking at Logan, he can see the determination in her blue eyes. "You take Fiona to pick up her things from the B&B, I'll phone Caroline to make arrangements at the Lovett, and we'll see where we go from there!"

"The Lovett...?" Fiona frowns in confusion.

"I think what Catherine meant to say, is that we would like you to stay there as our guest," Logan clarifies.

"That's what I said," Catherine's eyes widen obliviously.

When Logan returns from settling Mrs Richerson in at The Lovett Hotel, he finds Catherine in his home office already tapping away at the keyboard of her laptop.

"So..." he walks over to stand behind her chair, "...you've already made up your mind."

It isn't that Logan doesn't feel for the woman, or the young couple that have gone missing, but he is concerned for Catherine's health, and ultimately for the health of their unborn children.

Giving a noncommittal shrug of her slender shoulders, Catherine pulls up some interesting pictures that she has already found. "I'm just doing a bit of digging – just trying to see if there's anything to make my mind up about."

Deciding not to push the point, Logan watches the slideshow of gruesome discoveries that Catherine has set in motion.

"You see, these are all couples who have gone missing. Some of them have never been found, some were found murdered, and some were thought to have committed suicide together." She looks up over her shoulder to Logan, "I so do not get that!"

Logan leans forward to wrap her in his warmth and love, "I saw how difficult it was for my father – watching the woman he loved become so ill and then to be faced with the rest of his life without her...well..." Logan hugs Catherine and lays his cheek on her hair, "I can't imagine my life without you, Catherine – I think for some people that is just too much!"

Laying her cheek against the strength of the arms that enfold her, Catherine has to concede that nothing is ever black and white. "Clearly...and I know it's wrong to judge people, it just seems such a terrible waste."

Swiveling her chair so that she is properly facing him, Logan looks deep into Catherine's troubled blue eyes. "If you do this, it will hurt you, and you'll wear yourself out — remember our boys, they need you fit and strong to nurture and bring them into this world."

A sad shadow passes over Catherine's face, "If it were one of them, Andrew or Adam, missing with their girlfriend...wouldn't we beg someone to help us find them?"

For a long moment Logan can only stare. *This is Catherine, the troubled yet wonderful woman who cares about people more deeply than most...and I love her so much. I can't force her to turn away from this — she'll only worry herself into illness if I do!*

"It's your decision, I'll support you whichever way you decide to go." Placing a kiss on her upturned lips, Logan gives her an encouraging smile.

"Really?" she asks,

"Really!"

CHAPTER THREE

Actually going into the office is a rarity for Catherine these days. Logan prefers her to work from home, as he is deliberately doing more often himself.

It isn't that he is worried for her and the children she is carrying in any specific area, but he knows that she will overwork if he isn't there to call time for a break or rest period – and she doesn't have a bed she can take a nap on at the office.

Parking her lovely blue sports car in the office car park, Catherine finds she is struggling more and more to get out of the low slung car. It definitely wasn't designed with pregnant women in mind.

"Hey, Catherine," Susie, the new receptionist, greets her. "I didn't know you were coming in today – should I get lunch in for you later when I get some for the others?"

"Mmm," Catherine narrows her eyes at Susie, "no thanks, and you are not here to wait on that lot," and shoots an arm out to point in the direction of the inner offices. "If they are taking advantage of you, just give me a heads up and I'll sort it."

Smiling brightly, Susie thanks her, "Oh, that's alright, and thanks for the support, but it was my idea. I always go to the same place to pick up a plated lunch – I just offered to bring some back when Emma said she liked the look of mine."

Nodding, Catherine continues on her way, "Ok then; just don't let them get you running private errands for them." *I know Ben of old, if he can get someone else to do jobs he doesn't particularly want to do he will. Like I used to when we first teamed up - what a charmer, half the time I didn't even realise I was being manipulated. But he's good at tech stuff and now he's a partner he won't want to be wasting resources any more than I do.*

Susie must have rung through to Ben to let him know that Catherine has come in, as he walks out to greet her before she reaches her own office.

"Hey, does Logan know you're here?" Ben asks, pulling Catherine in for a casual hug.

"He's not my keeper!" she snaps back, then smiles to soften her words. "Though he's doing a damn fine impersonation," Catherine concedes. "And yes, he does know I'm here – I need to have a word with you."

A curious look comes into Ben's grey eyes, "Intriguing – is it work or private?" he asks while guiding her into his office and pulling up the visitor's chair.

Shutting the door behind them, Catherine takes the visitor's seat and tells Ben about the unexpected visitor at the house. "The poor woman is out of her mind," she continues after filling him in on the background. "I haven't seen her today, yet, but I spoke to Caroline and she tells me that Fiona is settled in and had breakfast in her room."

"Are you picking up the tab for that?" Ben asks cautiously.

"Yes, but it won't go through the business," she snaps. "You won't lose any of your precious profits."

"Well, good," Ben frowns, "though that wasn't why I was asking." His frown deepens, "I was just wondering how deep your involvement is – after all, you don't actually know this woman or the missing kids, why get involved?" *I bet Logan isn't too keen. If you try doing what I think you're going to, he won't be keen at all!*

"I don't know how involved I am," Catherine tells him honestly. "At least, I'm not sure how involved I can be." Getting up to pace the room, Catherine tries to put into words her conflicting wants, needs and emotions. "My gut tells me to say no, not to get involved in something that, as Logan has already pointed out, will tire me out and could put our babies at risk."

"But..." Ben prompts when Catherine falls silent.

"But what if it were one of them missing out there with no one to give a damn about what is happening to them; except a frantic parent who has absolutely no idea what to do to help them!" Slumping back down onto the chair, Catherine rubs her hands over her tired face – she hadn't slept well after Fiona's visit.

"Hmm, it seems your heart is winning out over your gut," Ben smiles ruefully. "Obviously Logan has some concerns, but you could win him over if you really want to," he tells her. "So, do you really want to?" he asks when she frowns.

"Yes, I think I do," she admits, to him and to herself. I don't know why I didn't just say yes in the first place – there's no way I can walk away from this...from them!"

"So what do you need?" he asks pleasantly, already resigned to her decision. "We can handle the workload." Ben gives an uncomfortable grimace, "David is brilliant; though I would appreciate you not telling him I said that."

Catherine laughs, already relaxing now that her decision has been made. "And Emma, is she brilliant?"

A grin spreads across Ben's handsome features, "And then some."

"I meant at work," Catherine finds herself blushing, still not comfortable with sex talk.

"That's what I meant," Ben widens his eyes innocently. "Can I help that you have a dirty mind since you got yourself married?"

"I do not have a dirty mind," Catherine denies, her cheeks flaming even hotter and giving an indignant huff. "Can we just get back to the business in hand?!"

"Which is...?" Ben asks, just as a knock sounds on his closed office door, which Emma opens and puts her head through.

"Natalie and Joshua," Catherine replies, just as Emma steps fully into the room.

"Oh, isn't that the names of the lovely young couple who have gone missing?" Emma asks curiously.

Looking up at the younger woman, Catherine realises she doesn't know her very well, having not worked in the office very much since her arrival.

"It is; what do you know about them?" she asks casually.

"Oh, nothing really," Emma smiles, "just what I read in the newspapers. It's awful," she elaborates, "to think that they just disappeared off the side of a hill they were climbing. And in broad daylight," she adds with an air of incredulity.

"Awful," Catherine echoes. "I had Natalie's mum at my door last night, asking for my help to find them."

It was Emma's turn to go wide eyed. "Why? Do you know her?"

Shaking her head, Catherine sighs, "Not at all, but she had that stupid article the newspapers ran about the Charlie Edwards trial. It had a bit in it that acknowledged mine and Logan's participation in finding and capturing the murdering ba..." Catherine remembers herself just in time. Rolling her eyes she looks down at her growing belly and gives a despairing shake of her head.

"You're getting better at that," Ben tells Catherine. "There was a time you couldn't form a sentence without some form of profanity in it."

Narrowing her eyes, Catherine gives Ben a withering look. "I'm still the boss around here, just don't get too cocky."

Emma steps in to defuse what could turn into a heated argument. "So you're going to help her? Wow, that would be really interesting," she adds at Catherine's nod.

Standing, Catherine eyes the younger woman speculatively. But before she can voice her thoughts, Ben interjects.

"No! No, Catherine...," he states firmly, "...you cannot poach my staff to work on your pet project!"

"Didn't we just establish that I am the boss around here," she glares down at Ben. "But, no, I won't be poaching MY staff to work on my 'pet project', as you so call it." Then she turns back to Emma, who now looks crestfallen, "But if you want to give some of your free time to helping me, I'd welcome it."

Eyes brightening instantly, Emma readily agrees, "You bet, when do we start?"

Giving a low chuckle, Catherine remembers being just this eager when she started out in computing – but then she had been eleven at the time. *It started out of boredom and became my life – and it kept me out of trouble in the Psyc' home and then it came in handy when I moved into foster care!*

"You've got my mobile number – just give me a ring when you're ready to start," Catherine gives Emma an appreciative smile. "But be prepared, once you start on this it will probably take over everything else. It kind'a becomes addictive till it's finished."

"I bet," Emma grins, obviously not put off. "When will you be starting – or have you already?"

Ben gives a snort of disgust, "Well of course she's already started," he states with a shake of his head. "I'll bet the mother hadn't left the house before she started planning her strategy. And I'll bet you didn't get to bed before doing some work on the computer...?" When he sees Catherine's cheeks pink, he gives a loud, "Ha! I knew it!"

"Well, Mr Know-it-all, if you've finished ragging on me, I just came to let you know I will continue to oversee any new work proposals but I won't be taking an active role in them for the time being." Catherine looks at him steadily, gauging Ben's reaction. "Will you be able to manage without me for a while?"

Giving a quick roll of his eyes and a tut of disgust, Ben looks over at Emma when he gives his reply. "I think we can manage, don't you?"

Emma beams, "We'll be fine, and given the work you'll be doing, it'll be a pleasure to help out in any way I can."

Driving over to The Lovett, Catherine considers her options and decides to discuss her plans with her sister before having a chat with Fiona Richerson.

The hotel gardens are in impeccable order, as usual. The hot summer is bringing all the flowers out in full bloom and it makes a colourful frontage to the beautiful old hotel.

Giving a wave to the receptionist, Catherine makes her way over to the private penthouse lift and punches the button. When the doors open she steps in and looks at herself in the reflective surface of the doors.

Her previously close cropped hair has grown out into a short, slightly wavy look that seems to compliment her face. Not that Catherine knows about such things, but Logan, and her sisters, have told her as much – and looking at herself in the lift doors she can't find anything to disagree with that.

She is wearing her favourite lemon dress today – Catherine likes it so much that she asked Vanessa Shelby, its designer, if it could be made in blue, lavender and an autumnal rust colour. Her wardrobe has changed completely from the meagre jog bottoms and baggy tops that she used to buy from the local charity shops. Logan has been instrumental in that change, and many others, she smiles to herself – and is still smiling when the lift doors open into the Penthouse lounge.

"Well, you look happy," Caroline grins and pulls Catherine in for a sisterly hug. "Now put me out of my misery, you sounded so intriguing when you phoned."

"Don't I get a coffee first?" Catherine smiles and returns her identical twin sister's hug.

"Already taken care of," Caroline tells her, and waves a hand toward the tray seated on the small occasional table between the luxurious settees. "I'll pour while you tell me what's been going on. Is this about the young couple who are missing – Mrs Richerson's daughter and her boyfriend? Have you decided to do it?"

Sinking into the softly sprung settee, Catherine takes the coffee her sister is holding out to her and gives a nod of her head. "I couldn't live with myself if they turned up dead and I hadn't done all I could to help find them," she sighs heavily.

Caroline looks concerned. "That could still happen, whether you help or not. Are you prepared for that?"

"I think I am," Catherine nods and sips at her coffee. "But I'm not sure Fiona Richerson is. She seems to be counting on me finding them in time – on me bringing them home safe and sound."

For a second or two, Caroline just looks into her drink, contemplating that thought. "You need to be straight with her," she tells Catherine eventually. "It'll be tough to do; we could do it together after this coffee if you like?"

Feeling the great weight of apprehension lift, Catherine nods, "That'd be great. Have you spoken to her much since Logan brought her over?"

"I sat with her for a while when she first arrived. That poor woman is going through such agonies trying not to think what might be happening to Natalie and her boyfriend," Caroline observes sympathetically. "And I'm trying not to empathise too much – I just can't bear to think of my own daughters being in Natalie's situation." She gives a shudder and both girls find themselves stroking their stomachs protectively.

Finishing up their drinks, the girls clear the table and put the tray on the dumb waiter to send it down to the hotel kitchen.

"No time like the present," Catherine tilts her head questioningly at her sister.

"Absolutely, let's get this over with."

When they get down to the ground floor, Caroline crosses the foyer to reception and checks whether Fiona Richerson has gone out, but is told no, not to their knowledge.

"Ok, ready?" she eyes Catherine as they go towards the lift.

With a wordless nod, Catherine follows beside her sister and then steps on to the lift when its doors open ominously before them.

"Jesus lifts are weird," Catherine shudders, "I always feel like I'm stepping into a mouth that's going to swallow me up."

Caroline laughs and gives her sister a comical frown. "You know...the shrinks would have a field-day with that little gem!"

"Yeah, wouldn't they just!" *Good job I didn't open my mouth when I was in the psychiatric unit, they would have kept me locked up for life!*

"Just a minute," they hear Fiona call out when a moment later Caroline knocks on her door. Then they hear the door being opened and Fiona Richerson peaks around it to see who is calling on her. "Oh, my dears please come in," she smiles in welcome. "But you'll have to excuse the mess, I've been trawling through all the newspapers for anything related to Natalie and Joshua. It's only been a week and already the story is fading into obscurity. No one seems interested in two teenagers who everyone assumes have run off together." Her sigh is heartbreaking to hear and Caroline instinctively crosses to put an arm around the woman's shoulders.

"That's why we're here," Caroline smiles, "Catherine is going to do everything she can to help find them." She guides Fiona to a seat and sits beside her to offer comfort. "We just want to make sure you understand what that means."

Fiona's face goes from excited to confused in the blink of an eye. "I'm not really sure I understand you," Fiona frowns.

Catherine sits in a nearby armchair and leans forward. "It's just that, I want to help, I even have a volunteer from work who is willing to help in her spare time," she begins tentatively. "I just don't want to get your hopes up – I'll do my best but..." Catherine's voice tails off, unable to finish the thought.

Fiona nods, the penny dropping with a loud thud in her head. Reaching over she puts a hand over Catherine's, "You're a good girl, and I'm certain you'll do your best, but I'm not addle brained...I know my Natalie and her Joshua might never come home."

Catherine lets out a breath she hadn't realised she was holding. "You are the bravest woman I have ever met. I'm just...in awe – I hope I can be half the mum to my boys that you are to Natalie. She's a lucky girl."

"Nonsense," Fiona pats Catherine's hand and turns to include Caroline in her sentiment. "You girls will be wonderful mothers – you already have heaps of love and compassion, which are the basic tools for excellent parenting."

On the drive back home Catherine can't help thinking of Fiona. *She hasn't given up hope but she's trying to keep it real. Though I don't know how...just the thought of Andrew or Adam coming to harm... It can't happen, I have to find Natalie and Joshua before they come to harm. That's just how it has to be!*

CHAPTER FOUR

By midnight, Catherine is getting her second wind. Logan had accepted her decision to help Fiona as he'd promised, but not without voicing a few reservations.

When she got back from her visit with Fiona, Catherine had waited for Logan to get home from his office and they had discussed her options.

As far as Catherine was concerned, she didn't have any. There was no way she could walk away from Natalie, Joshua or Fiona. This wasn't just a story in a newspaper anymore; she was involved and had been asked for help, and knowing what she was capable of she couldn't refuse that plea.

But Logan had some serious reservations. "I knew you would take this on," he had told her quietly, "you could never turn your back on anyone who needed your help.

But it has to be different this time," he'd stated firmly. "You can't stay up till all hours, eating only when you remember and sleeping only when you're fit to drop."

He hadn't been angry, but Logan had been very concerned. "You and our children need to come first – if we look after your health theirs will follow."

Now he was in the shower and had given her until he got out of it to wrap things up.

She'd spent most of the evening sifting through police files trying to find out everything they had. As far as Catherine could see, Fiona had been right, they weren't looking too hard: a few interviews with friends of Natalie's and Joshua's, a couple of work interviews and some from the rambling club they were both members of. But the police had come up with zilch!

When Catherine looks up Logan is stood in the doorway with one towel slung low around his hips and another in his hands still towelling off his hair.

His arm muscles bulk up with the action and his chest and abdo muscles ripple enticingly. She might be pregnant, but Catherine is still able to appreciate the all-male figure of her husband – and decides she wants some of that.

Logan watches Catherine close the lid of her laptop, noticing that her eyes haven't left him. *Christ those eyes are sexy...the way they devour, I feel hot already.* And looking down at the towel at his hips, Logan smiles at the giveaway bulge beneath it.

"Well, well, well." Catherine rounds the desk and walks over to him, looking directly at that bulge. "I gather you're shower perked you up!"

Giving a sexy chuckle, Logan holds his arms out towards her and makes to pull her in for a hug. But Catherine evades him and snags the towel away.

"Definitely all perked up," she smiles salaciously. As Logan stands watching her playful actions, Catherine walks around him as if admiring a work of art. "You are so damn gorgeous," she tells him. "All toned muscle, and just look at that peachy arse!" With that she gives it a short, sharp smack, then bends to kiss it better. But then she drops to her knees, "One bite just isn't enough," she tells him and nibbles on one firm buttock then the other. "What a body...and it belongs to me, every lovely rippling inch of it."

Not stopping her feast, Catherine reaches round front and hears him groan as she takes him in her hand. It's a heady feeling to make a man like Logan tremble, but that is just what he is doing under her ministrations.

"Do a 180," she instructs lustily, her voice deep and warm with longing, "I'm ready for the main meal."

Logan does as he's told and Catherine takes him in on a long lusty sigh. Gently at first, slow and teasing, she moves her lips and tongue up and down the hard length of him then causes Logan to cry out when she suddenly swallows him whole and sucks with everything she has.

That loud cry fires Catherine, and she works him hard till he's right on the edge. She can feel his hips and thighs tighten, knows that if she continues she'll be drinking his seed, and Catherine has other plans for that.

Getting to her feet, it's Catherine's turn to gasp. Logan pulls her into his arms and kisses her with a passion that is red hot and getting hotter by the second.

With a deft swipe of his arm behind Catherine's already weak knees, Logan swings her up into his arms without even breaking the kiss. Then he lifts his head to look down at her, "I'm taking you to bed, wife, and once there I'm going to make love to you so thoroughly you won't dream about anything but me tonight."

And he doesn't disappoint. Catherine is quickly undressed and finds herself lying beneath Logan before she can think. His mouth is doing unbelievably wonderful things to her breasts, her nipples, her earlobes...and the words he is using are so graphic her body vibrates with anticipation.

When he moves down to taste her, to thrust his expert tongue into her center, it is her turn to cry out. Her fingers tangle in his hair, her hands holding him to her, desperate for the pleasure his mouth gives her.

Then she bows, her back lifting from the bed, her thighs clamping together on either side of Logan's head as her body convulses on an orgasm that goes on and on.

Before she can recover, Logan pushes into her. Holding her buttocks off the bed he thrusts deeply. Repeatedly.

At first Catherine had been wary of sex during pregnancy, but had researched it on her trusty computer and found out that sex was rarely thought to be a factor in miscarriages after twelve weeks, and she is now twenty-six weeks.

Their cries of release are loud and come from their hearts as well as their loins. Lowering his body to the bed, Logan rolls to bring Catherine to lie atop him and she shifts her position for comfort.

Their hearts beat a joint tattoo against their ribs, their contented smiles identical, and their love so deep and warm they are basking in it languorously.

His large gentle hand strokes down her back, cups her bottom then moves back up. He does this again and again, loving the feel of this incredible woman in his arms.

My wife! My wife and soon to be the mother of our children – how could I ever want for more! Impossible!

"I think you're right," Catherine lifts her head and turns into his wonderfully broad chest to kiss the muscles that are still trembling, "I'll be dreaming about that all night. You are such a stud! I bet I could make millions just hiring you out!"

Giving a bellowing laugh, Logan has to wrap Catherine in his strong arms to stop her from toppling off of him as he shakes with mirth.

"So, you'd be willing to share me, would you?" he smiles and kisses the top of her head.

"Not on your life," Catherine tells him more seriously. "Your mine, and I'm yours, and that's just how it is. Forever!" *I won't lose you. I will not muck this up!*

Moving her to lie beside him, Logan draws Catherine against his chest, spooning snugly, a perfect fit.

"That's a vow I'll take to my grave," Logan whispers against her hair. "And it's one that will be a pleasure to live by, for all eternity and beyond."

"You really love me...don't you?" Catherine states in wonder, and feels his strong arms tighten about her.

"More than you know," he whispers against her silky soft hair. "There aren't sufficient words to tell you how I feel. I'm the luckiest man alive, and that's a fact!"

Her dreams are sweet, Catherine and Logan with their boys at Lakelands; Henry laughing, with his knees crossed bouncing them in turn as they sit on his foot while he holds their outstretched hands. 'Gee up granddad' she hears them squeal with delight.

When she wakes, Catherine is lost in thought. Her dream was so vivid, she had seen her boys' faces, and unsurprisingly they had looked the image of Logan as a boy.

But it was the sense of 'family' that was causing her to wonder. She had never had that, had never experienced love in all those multi-faceted ways that families do.

The love of a dad for his daughter; she is still trying to wrap her head and her heart around that with Tom. She has only recently found her father, the man she'd believed, all of her life, had deserted both her and her mother. It had filled her with loathing for him, had served to make her bitter and hard hearted, keeping everyone at a distance, far enough away that they couldn't hurt her.

And the love of a sister or brother – she hadn't even known she had any. During her two years in a psychiatric unit, after being forced to watch her mother's torture murder, Catherine had separated herself from everyone around her, both mentally and physically. She hadn't spoken a word in all the time she was there.

As she had told Logan, when he'd asked her about that part of her life, she hadn't even tried to speak because there was nothing to say. She had been forced to watch the only person who had ever loved her being ripped from her life in the worst way possible; words were useless after that.

Foster care had been one long passage of time, like a survival test that you either excelled at or fell victim to. Her time in 'the system' had hardened an already tough shell of armour; she didn't suffer fools gladly and trusted them even less.

Her exceptional IQ had always been a yoke around her neck – the other kids called her freak, pointing and staring all the time. But in the end, it was what had kept her sane.

All the books, her computer skills that she developed very early on, and her ability to lose herself in anything she did, had kept her separate from the hurt. The world. The pain. The love.

"You're quiet this morning," Logan observes over breakfast in the conservatory. "Is something worrying you?"

"Do you miss your father?" Catherine asks instead of answering Logan's question.

Raising his eyebrows at this bolt from the blue, Logan considers her question. "Yes, in many ways and at the oddest times," he tells her with a wistful smile.

"Then why did you leave? Why move to Sheriton when you could have lived at Lakelands?" she asks, bewildered at the thought.

"Well, I never did leave, exactly," Logan tries to explain. "It was more a case of not ever moving back." Watching Catherine frown, he continues, "I went off to university and life just took me on a journey that ended up in Sheriton. It was never a conscious decision, more a gradual transition. Why do you ask?"

Watching him intently, Catherine can't imagine ever feeling as confident or as sure of herself as Logan appears to be right now.

"Henry loves you," she states softly, her eyes having never left Logan's, "and you left him behind."

"Hardly." Logan shifts with discomfort. "I just left the nest as all fledglings must." He narrows his eyes and really looks at Catherine. "You're in a strange mood this morning; what is all this about?"

Giving him an unconvincing smile, Catherine pushes up from the table, having eaten very little breakfast. "I'm just broody, I suppose. Will you be going into work this morning?" she asks, changing the subject adroitly.

His frown only slowly disappears as Logan decides to allow the subject change to go unchallenged. "If you're feeling ok, I thought I would," he tells her, none too sure that Catherine is alright, but unable to put his finger on why.

"Ok then. We'll be occupying your home office for the day," she tells him, her hands smoothing over her baby bump lovingly.

Standing, Logan moves over to Catherine and puts gentle hands on either shoulder. "Don't tire yourself out. I know how important what you're doing is to you, but please...remember to take a rest on the bed." With that he leans down to place a tender kiss on her forehead and draws her into the warmth of his arms. *What is wrong? Something is definitely troubling you?*

By midafternoon Catherine is starting to flag. Mrs Baines had brought her midday meal up and she had managed to eat every bite. But her work on trying to locate the missing couple is not going well so she is loath to take a rest, feeling that she hasn't earned one yet.

I can't overdo things on the first day, Logan will be furious if he comes home and I'm wiped out.

Shutting everything down, Catherine goes through to the bedroom for a lie down. Her eyes close and she is fast asleep almost before her head hits the pillows.

She dreams of Lakelands, the beautiful grounds, the spacious house, and two little boys running around having the time of their lives.

Henry looks happy, almost rejuvenated by the family that surrounds him. Logan, too, looks happy and content, his boys the pride of his life and the greatest joy he's ever known.

Only Catherine is missing from the idyllic scene. But then she sees herself walk out onto the veranda, her smile as wide as everyone else's and looking just as content.

They are a family, all of them together, and so happy - like nothing Catherine has ever experienced in her own life.

"Catherine, wake up now." Logan is gently shaking her shoulders. "Wake up, sweetheart - I'm here, no need to cry."

She can hear Logan's voice, can feel him shaking her awake, but Catherine doesn't want to wake up, doesn't want to leave the wonderful dream.

Logan holds Catherine to him, rocking her gently awake and feels her tears continue to soak into his shirt.

"I knew I shouldn't have left you - you were in such a strange mood this morning."

"I'm sorry," Catherine tries to stem the flow of tears, but is woefully unsuccessful. "It was just so lovely, and we were all so happy," she tells him, making no sense at all to Logan.

"In your dream?" he asks uncertainly. When she nods her head against his chest, Logan still doesn't have a clue what's going on. "Then, why are you crying - that sounds like a pretty good dream to me?"

Sniffing in a most unladylike way, Catherine moves her head to look up at him, "But he's all alone, and too proud to let anyone know how lonely he really is."

Wide eyed with sudden understanding, Logan passes Catherine a handkerchief and waits for her to dry her eyes.

"You're talking about my father, aren't you?" Logan asks, still none the wiser as to why this should bring Catherine to tears.

Nodding again, she uses the handkerchief that Logan has given her to tidy herself up and moves a little away from him.

"That first time you took me to Lakelands," and the beginning of a smile tugs at her still trembling lips, "do you remember, after that ridiculous shopping trip you took me on?" Logan nods, his smile full and bright. "Well, I caught Henry looking through a large book of original blueprints for the house." Catherine looks a little shame faced but continues, "I actually promised I wouldn't tell you this, so I hope Henry will forgive me."

Looking confused now, Logan says, "You promised my father not to tell me that he was looking at the house blueprints – why on earth would he ask you not to tell me that?"

"Because...he was looking for ways to modernise the house in the hopes of you coming home someday," she tails off sadly.

Getting to his feet, Logan paces the bedroom trying to get his head round this information.

Pushing a restless hand through his longer than usual hair, he finally comes to a stop in front of the bed. Looking down at Catherine he begins to nod, "You want us to move to Lakelands."

It was more of a statement than a question, but Catherine nods silently.

Again Logan turns and paces the room before coming back to Catherine, finally sitting back down next to her on the bed. "Have you really thought about this? I mean, other than in dreams," he smiles encouragingly.

Surprising him, she shakes her head, "No, actually. Both times the notion came from dreams – first last night and then just now, but I don't think that's a reason to dismiss the idea," she asserts when Logan's expression turns sceptical.

"Well, I suggest we both give it some serious thought before we go packing up lock stock and barrel to go live with my father," he states, not unkindly. Pulling her into a fierce hug, Logan lays his cheek on the top of her sleep tousled hair. "You do know, most wives would run a mile from their in-laws," and she can feel his smile against her head and gives an answering smile. "Yet here you are wanting to move in with them – or him, I should say."

There was a note of sadness in Logan's voice, and Catherine heard it. "I'm sorry; you must miss your mum and going back might make that harder," she tells him, and looks up to see his face before Logan can hide his pain.

Giving a sigh, he pulls her against him and rubs her back gently, comforting himself as much as giving comfort to Catherine. "She was a great woman," he begins softly, "and a wonderful mother; you remind me of her often," he surprises her, and has to tighten his hold to stop Catherine from springing away from him. "Shh, I just meant your intuitive thinking, and your generous heart – she had those in spades and used them well."

Waiting for him to continue, Catherine bites her bottom lip nervously when he doesn't. "You never really speak about her, and I don't ask because I don't want to hurt you."

Logan continues to hold her in silence, gently rocking her back and forth while his large hand strokes gently up and down her back.

"Let's go for a walk, it's still warm outside," he invites quietly.

Looking up at him, now that his strong arms have released their hold on her, Catherine smiles shyly, "I'd like that."

For all their time together, this feels like the most intimate to Catherine - Logan, asking her to walk with him while obviously contemplating letting her in to his most private thoughts and feelings about his mother.

After stopping in the kitchen to get them both a glass of fresh orange juice from the fridge, Logan takes Catherine's hand and leads her out to the bench near the fishpond.

For a moment, or three, they sit in silence and Catherine begins to wonder if Logan can actually bring himself to talk of Ellie, his mother.

"She was so funny," he begins suddenly, and Catherine feels herself start. "My mother had a wicked sense of humour and loved to laugh – she said it was what kept her heart young," and he turns to smile at Catherine.

"I think that was what first drew me to you," he tells her with a considering tilt of his head.

Almost gagging on her juice, Catherine looks up at him with incredulous eyes, "We met in Arthur's office and I definitely did not laugh!"

Leaning back against the bench, Logan gives a bellowing laugh at her indignant denial. "Don't get defensive," he tells her and pulls her to sit back with him. "I'm talking about the way you greeted Arthur — your smile was so warm and genuine, not an ounce of pretence or sales smarm about it."

"I don't do 'sales smarm'," she frowns, wriggling to get comfortable as Logan's arm comes over her shoulders to pull her in closer. "I like Arthur and Robert, too. They both deal with people in a no-nonsense way that gets right down to business without making superficial judgements. I like that," she adds simply.

"Hmm," Logan gives a deep hum in his throat at the mention of Catherine liking Robert. "Arthur always regarded you with deep affection, in a fatherly way I think," he tells her kindly, but his voice changes when he refers to Robert. "Robert, however, had other ideas. He wanted you as badly as I did; I saw that right off the bat. So I knew I had to move fast."

"He's married to my sister," Catherine reminds him with a satisfied smile. "And you're the only man for me," she states, giving him a playful poke in the ribs.

His arm tightens over her shoulders. "And you're the only woman for me," he sighs, his contentment settling his moment of jealousy. "That's just how it was for my parent's too. I never saw either of them look at each other with anything less than the deepest love – even when they were angry."

"Well, that's hard to imagine." Catherine frowns at the thought. "I mean, isn't that the point of being angry – like, at this moment in time I hate your guts so get out of my face!"

Giving a low chuckle, Logan gives her shoulders another hug. "That might be what you mean, but even then I don't think that would be true."

"Now you've got me totally confused," Catherine admits with her brows knit.

"You love me," he states, and laughs when Catherine gives a snort of disgust at his cocky statement. "You know you do, and when you get mad that love doesn't just disappear. I can still see it in your eyes even when they're spitting fire and brimstone at me."

Catherine does manage to pull out of his arm then, and turns to frown up at him. "Fire and brimstone is witch stuff – are you calling me a witch?!"

"You see," he chuckles, causing her frown to deepen, "you're mad at me, but you still love me. I can see it even though you're doing a good impression of someone who wants to punch my lights out."

Then suddenly, all her rush of temper evaporates. "Your right!" she states, then giggles at his comical look of shock. "I admit when I'm wrong," she tells him, and punches his arm to punctuate the point.

"Well then, I congratulate you, I don't think I ever heard my mother utter those exact words," and the distant smile of remembering is back. "She would say things like 'I see your point, but' or 'that could work too, but' or even, 'isn't that what I said in the first place' when she would try to convince dad that he was the one who had misunderstood and it had been her idea all along."

Catherine's smile is full and adoring, her husband looks so handsome and devoted to a mother he can't share his present happiness with.

"You miss her more than you let on," she tells him.

Nodding, Logan concedes that she is right. "I do, and more especially so just now."

Laying a hand on her baby bump, Catherine looks down then back at Logan. "The children – you wish she was around to meet them, and give them the same love she gave to you."

"Yes," his sigh is one of regret rather than sadness, "and you too. She would have loved you," he grins, surprising her.

"You think?" she asks sceptically.

"Mmm, I do," he tells her sincerely, "just as much as my father does."

Her eyes fill, and her bottom lip trembles dangerously. "That's so nice."

Catherine isn't used to 'nice' in her life. Until Logan, her life had been filled with torment, grief and work. She hadn't let anyone close enough to see her feelings, let alone hurt them. But people often had anyway – with their negative judgements and condescension, they had managed to hurt her pretty badly.

His hand reaches out to cup her cheek gently. "You deserve much better than 'nice'," and his loving smile gives Catherine everything she needs to make the past the past and the present her very happy future.

"I love you, Logan. I know I don't say that often enough, but I don't want the words to ever be just something we say," and she raises a hand to cover his on her cheek. "I love you, and I'm so proud to be carrying your children."

Pulling her back into his arms, Logan whispers, "Yes, my mother would have loved you."

CHAPTER FIVE

Wherever they are being kept, Natalie and Joshua are freezing – but at least they are alive and they're together.

Natalie doesn't know how she would have stayed sane this long without Joshua. When the screams come they are terrible and seem to last for hours.

Mostly they sound like women's screams, or pleas for someone to stop whatever is being done to them. But sometimes they are male, again pleading for whomever to stop what they are doing, or even, at one point, threatening to kill the son-of-a-bitch if he doesn't.

"I think there must be more couples like us," Joshua observes in the darkness. "That madman must have abducted them like he did us, but I haven't heard the first couple for a while now – you know...the ones we heard on our first night here."

"Yes," Natalie agrees, "he has a strong Yorkshire accent and she is from up north too."

They fall silent, both trying not to think the worst or at least trying not to voice their worries out loud. That would make them real, the possible terror more tangible somehow.

But Natalie can't stop herself from asking, "Do you think he'll come for us soon – we've been here a week now, he must have brought us here for a reason?"

Joshua puts an arm around Natalie's shoulders and feels her tremble with fear. "We have to stay positive – someone is looking for us, they will find us before he gets around to noticing us," he states more confidently than he actually feels. "If we stay quiet, make no noise or trouble that will attract attention, he may even forget that we're here."

Then the screams begin again, a woman terrified and sobbing. "Let me go – no, please, no more, no more...aaaahhhhhhhhhh!"

And then a man - angry, frustrated and rattling cage doors, "You bastard! Let her go! Let her go! I'll kill you, you twisted fuck! I'll kill you!"

At breakfast next morning, Catherine and Logan are both in a good mood. The frank talk they'd had the night before seems to have cleared the air and made each of them feel lighter.

"I think I'll drive into the office today," Catherine smiles brightly over at Logan. "I want a quick word with Emma — I can't remember if I told you that she volunteered to help me with the search for Natalie and Joshua."

Nodding, Logan returns her smile. "Good, that will lighten the load and help you to get some rest," he tells her. "I'll bet you felt as guilty as hell tearing yourself away from your computer to take a rest on the bed yesterday — with Emma helping you won't need to feel that way."

"You're right, on both counts," Catherine chuckles softly. "You know me too well."

Leaning across the table to take Catherine's hand and pull her closer, Logan gives her a brief kiss." Just remember that when you try to pull the wool over my eyes — I can tell when you're hiding something, you go all quiet and pensive, and look guilty as hell."

Scowling deeply, Catherine gives Logan the evil eye. "I can keep a secret if I really want to," and lifts her chin defiantly, "I just don't choose to!"

Taking a pile of proposals that she has gone through into the office with her, Catherine makes herself a mug of her favourite hot chocolate drink before going through to David and Emma's office.

"Hi David," she greets the young man who Ben recruited fresh out of university when she had been busy trying to find her mother's murderer.

"Hello, Mrs Sayers," David smiles shyly.

He reminds Catherine of a character named 'Brains' in a children's programme she watched as a child.

"If you insist on calling me Mrs anything, it's Colson-Sayers," she corrects him with a smile. "There are no males to carry on the name so I tagged it together with Logan's when we married."

"S.sorry ab.bout that," David stutters uncomfortably. "It's a good i.idea th.though."

Catherine hands the pile of paperwork she brought with her over to David and asks him to take it through to Ben. "I've written a brief outline for each proposal – the ones I don't think we should take on are clearly marked, but ask Ben to look them all over and decide which ones he thinks you can all handle."

Blushing, David takes the pile held out to him, and leaves Catherine and Emma to talk.

Closing the office door, Catherine takes a seat near Emma and smiles a greeting. "I wanted a private word," she tells the young woman who was recruited by Ben at the same time as he'd found David.

"I gathered," grins Emma, who is at the opposite end of the spectrum to David in the confidence department, "and so did David."

"Well, hell, I tried to be discreet," Catherine grimaces uncomfortably. "I'm not a people person, you know that!"

"You do alright," and Emma gets up to help herself to a mug of black coffee from the coffee-maker. "I see you've got a mug of chocolate but there's plenty of coffee made if you decide you want one after that."

Nodding, Catherine decides to dive in with both feet. "Emma, did you mean it about helping me with the enquiry I'm running on the missing couple?"

Looking a bit taken aback, Emma says, "Of course – didn't I sound serious?"

"Yes...yes you did...it's just..." Catherine frowns, trying to find the right words to best voice her concerns without making Emma feel awkward. "Emma, I feel I should warn you...not all my methods are entirely legal." Frowning, she takes a sip of her chocolate. "Actually, most of what I do isn't legal at all – I just thought I should give you a heads up before you make a final decision to get involved."

Brows raised, Emma leans back in her chair to consider Catherine and then bursts out laughing. "You are so lovely," she tells her surprised boss. "You want my help yet you came here to warn me off."

Cheeks reddening, Catherine becomes agitated. "Well...damn it...yes I did!" she explodes. "I thought it was only fair to be upfront and not get you involved in something dodgy – I wish I'd saved my breath!" And Catherine pushes to her feet, turning to leave in a huff.

"Please wait," Emma also stands, and quickly rounds her desk to walk over to Catherine. "I wasn't laughing at you for being here – it was just..." It's Emma's turn to falter and struggle to find the right words. "It seems it didn't occur to you that I might already know that, to get the kind of information we'll need, we are going to have to hack into some pretty major systems."

"You already thought it through to that point?" Catherine asks, still not sure if she's mad at Emma for laughing at her.

"Catherine, it isn't on my CV because I really wanted this job, but...I was known at university for my hacking skills," she confesses, wincing at the possible consequences.

Then it's Emma's turn to be surprised when Catherine bursts into peals of laughter. "And here I was thinking you were straight-laced and whiter-than-white! Ha! Just goes to show," Catherine gives the younger woman a punch on her upper arm in solidarity, "you can't tell everything about a person just by looking."

Emma's mouth forms a wide 'O'. "Ow," she exclaims, and rubs the top of her arm where she's sure a bruise is forming as they speak.

"Oh, sorry," Catherine takes a step back. "It never seems to bother Logan when I do that."

Looking askance, Emma gives a low huff. "Logan is a man-mountain of solid muscle – trust me, to us mere mortals, you pack a mean punch!"

Catherine actually smiles with pride at that remark. "I'd say thank you, but then you might try to hit me back."

Both girls chuckle and, in that instant, become fast friends.

"So, tell me about your hacking days," Catherine asks as they retake their seats. "Did you ever get busted?"

"Not once," Emma states with pride, "but I know plenty who did. I learned from their mistakes and made sure to cover my tracks – or, I should say, I unpick my tracks so that I don't leave any behind."

Giving a nod of serious consideration, Catherine says, "That's good, very good, you're careful – so am I forgiven for disrespecting your mad skills?"

With a grin, Emma nods and raises her mug in salute. "To mad computer geeks and hackers; may we never get caught!"

While she's out and about, Catherine decides to drive over to Caroline's and see how her sister is doing. Last time she saw her was when they talked with Fiona Richerson, and that hadn't been the happiest of times.

She needs some family time, a few moments of normal before diving back into the twisted world of abductors and what they are likely to do to their abductees.

"Hey, sis', twice in one week," Caroline greets her, as Catherine steps off the private lift and into the penthouse of The Lovett Hotel. "Is this business or pleasure?"

Catherine grimaces, "By business, do you mean Natalie and Joshua?" At Caroline's nod, she shakes her head firmly. "No, actually, though I'll get right back on that the minute I leave here." Changing her mind about what she'd been about to say, Catherine instead says, "I'd kill for a cup of tea – you know, that fancy stuff that you drink...Lady something or other?"

"Lady Grey," Caroline provides, her brief frown indicating that she has picked up on Catherine's hesitation. "Travis prefers the Earl Grey, but I'm not so keen."

Giving a snort, Catherine flops down on a plush settee. "A regular his and hers – can I get a biscuit with that?"

With a narrowed stare, Caroline gives her twin the once over and decides that she looks a little peaky. "Did you eat lunch today?"

"Well...I... It wasn't that I forgot," Catherine eventually says, getting all defensive, "I just haven't had the time, yet."

"Then forget the biscuits, I'll order up some lunch," and crossing to the telephone, Caroline turns and asks, "what do you fancy?"

"I'm fine..." then seeing her sister's raised brow and look of impatience, Catherine changes her mind and says, "a salad, just something cold and easy."

After placing the order, Caroline walks back over to where Catherine is sat and sits with her feet up on the opposite settee. "Up, up, up," she waves a hand at her sister, indicating that she should adopt the same position.

"I'm not a damn dog," Catherine grumbles, but does as she's told.

"If you don't want me to tell Logan that you arrived here at two in the afternoon looking washed out and having missed lunch, then you'll behave and tell me what's wrong," Caroline threatens quietly.

Recognising the danger in that quiet tone from her own often barely controlled temper, Catherine decides that a few moments of embarrassment with Caroline are better than a row with Logan.

"Ok. Ok. God you're bossy! Heaven help your poor daughters!"

Catherine rolls her eyes when Caroline merely narrows hers. "I've been having weird dreams," she finally confesses. "Probably not weird to you, but definitely weird to me."

With eyes now rounded in speculation, Caroline turns to look at her twin full on. "Weird as in sexually deviant or nightmarish?"

"Neither," Catherine squirms uncomfortably. "The happy family kind," and rolls her eyes again when Caroline looks stumped.

"I didn't grow up in a happy family," Catherine states the obvious, her arms flailing and her voice rising, "so for me to dream about being part of one is weird...ok!"

"Ok."

"Ok then."

"So that's it?" Caroline asks bewildered when Catherine doesn't expand.

Pursing her lips, obviously deciding whether or not to elaborate, Catherine heaves a deciding sigh. "I think I want to go live with the in-laws," she tells her sister, as if it's a shameful idea that shouldn't be voiced out loud.

"You mean Henry...Logan's father?" Caroline enquires cautiously. And when her sister nods, she continues, "Well, I thought he was lovely when we met at the wedding – but why do you suddenly want to go live with the man?"

Abruptly getting up, Catherine starts pacing the room. "Because he's all alone in that huge house. Because his wife, the love of his life, is dead. Because his son went off to university and forgot to ever go home and I caught Henry looking at blueprints, racking his brains trying to think of a way to lure him back." Taking a deep breath after her rant, Catherine throws herself back down on the settee. "Because he's lonely, and he's nice, and I want my children to have a granddad in their lives," she finishes quietly. Wistfully. Sadly.

Caroline has to turn away to wipe at the tears that would only embarrass Catherine. At times like this she feels guilty for the happy childhood she spent with their father. True, she had never known their mother – but neither had she had to witness the rape and torture of the only person to ever love her, as Catherine had, and all at the tender age of nine.

Now here she was, opening up her damaged heart to make room in it for someone who, less than a year ago, she had never even met.

"I think that sounds wonderful," Caroline states softly, and manages to smile when Catherine's head jerks up and round to look at her. "And Lakelands isn't on the other side of the planet – you said it was only about an hour via the motorway and a few country roads."

Nodding, Catherine sits upright, looking at Caroline for any sign of a cover-up. "You really think it wouldn't be weird? I mean...Logan said most people run a mile from their in-laws."

"You are not most people," Caroline tells her gently, and crosses to Catherine to pull her in for a hug. "You have more love inside you than anyone I know. I'm proud that you're my sister."

"Well, damn!" and Catherine has to wipe a couple of tears away herself.

In the background the radio is playing softly. Until that moment Catherine hadn't even noticed it, but then she hears...

"Earlier today, the bodies of a male and a female were found on the Yorkshire moors. Police have stated that the bodies appear to have been there for about a week – the identities have as yet not been given out, but police believe they will be able to do so later today, after informing the next of kin!"

Catherine has gone white, her hand flying to hold her forehead. "I'm too late. Oh God, Caroline, I'm too late!"

CHAPTER SIX

Approaching Fiona Richerson's hotel room is one of the most difficult things Catherine has ever had to force herself to do.

Caroline had volunteered to accompany her, but Catherine had asked her to continue listening to the radio for further updates on the couple who have been found dead on the Yorkshire Moors.

Knocking on Fiona's hotel room door, Catherine takes a step back and waits with bated breath for the woman inside to open it.

When she does, Fiona is already talking on the telephone but waves Catherine inside.

Pacing the sitting room, Fiona listens to what someone is telling her on the other end of the line then slumps down onto the settee, silent tears beginning to fall.

"Yes, I see," she mumbles, and Catherine can only wait to find out what is going on. "But, I was hoping..." Again, Fiona is listening to what she is being told and nods in silent acquiescence. "I understand. Thank you."

Turning waterlogged eyes to Catherine, Fiona can only stare and shake her head wordlessly.

It's obvious to Catherine that the news is bad, but she can't figure out exactly what has been going on.

"Were you speaking to the police?" she asks Fiona, her heart plummeting into her boots at the other woman's silent nod. "Did they tell you they had made a positive ID?" Surprisingly, Fiona shakes her head.

Stumped now, Catherine decides she needs to ask a more direct question. "I need to know what they said then maybe I can help you."

Having retrieved a tissue from her handbag, Fiona dries her eyes and blows her nose then takes a couple of deep breaths.

"I was listening to the radio, I almost missed the announcement, and then I thought I must have misheard," Fiona stumbles through her explanation. "But I called the police, just to check if there was any news, and they told me about the young couple who have been found dead on the Yorkshire moors. But now they say they can't tell me anything else until they've made a formal identification." Her hands rise and fall helplessly in her lap, her eyes looking sad and hollow in her tired face.

Catherine's brows rise. "But they didn't ask you to come in to make an identification?"

Looking suddenly shocked, Fiona shakes her head. "That's odd, isn't it? If they thought they had found Natalie and Joshua wouldn't they have asked me to do that?"

Standing suddenly, Catherine holds out a hand to Fiona and helps her to her feet. "Come with me – I'd like to take you back to my home and put your mind at rest, or at least be able to give you some proper information."

"Alright," Fiona agrees cautiously. She wants to know if the couple on the moors is Natalie and Joshua, yet she's also very afraid.

A quick phone call to Caroline puts her in the picture, then Catherine ushers Fiona out of the hotel and into her car.

Neither woman speaks on the drive back to the house; both are lost in thoughts too awful to voice out loud.

Letting them in the front door, Catherine shows Fiona through to the kitchen where they find Mrs Baines preparing for the evening meal.

"Would you mind making Mrs Richerson a cup of tea?" Catherine asks, while guiding Fiona to a comfortable seat in the conservatory. "I'm going to be in Logan's office for a short while then I'll come back down and join you," she smiles at Fiona, trying to offer some small reassurance.

Racing up the stairs, Catherine fires up her laptop and gets to work. First she looks on the local police computer for updates on their investigation, and then the Derbyshire police computer for any updates there. Nothing!

Damn! Surely these police forces actually communicate with each other!

Another five minutes of rapid key crunching and she's on to something. Catherine has gone directly to the Yorkshire Police Department's computer and hacked in. There she browses through files and eventually finds the one she wants.

There are reports of the discovery of two naked bodies, one male, one female, and both in their late teens or early twenties. Then there is a witness statement from the young woman who made the gruesome discovery while out walking her dog.

Pictures...yes, let's have a look.

At first she can't take her eyes off the horrific injuries these two poor young people have suffered. The bruising covers around eighty percent of their bodies and is especially concentrated around the genitalia. The female has bite marks to her breasts, one nipple being almost bitten off.

It takes some effort for Catherine to continue, but she forces herself to click on more pictures until she finds some that clearly show the faces.

Not them! It's not them! Oh God, it isn't Natalie and Joshua!

But looking back at her computer screen, Catherine can't bring herself to be glad that it is this couple instead.

No one should have to die like that. Memories of her mother's suffering flash through her mind, the screams barely muffled by the silver duct tape he'd used to cover her mother's mouth. And the look of terror in her eyes is something Catherine will never forget.

"Is that how it was for you?" she asks, reaching a hand out to touch her fingers to the faces on her screen. "I'll find who did this to you – I swear I will!"

Shutting down her computer, Catherine returns downstairs to find Mrs Baines sat talking to Fiona about the lovely garden and how much she enjoys working for Catherine and Logan.

"Any more tea in that pot?" Catherine asks, as she walks over to the two women and takes a seat nearby.

"I'll fetch you a cup," Mrs Baines offers when she sees Catherine approach, and gives Fiona's hand a reassuring squeeze before going off to do so.

"It wasn't your daughter or Joshua who were found," Catherine immediately tells Fiona, and watches as the older woman sags back into her chair. "The police probably couldn't give you any information earlier until the official ID was made and, having looked at the photos, I can see why."

"Here you are then," Mrs Baines offers Catherine a steaming hot cup of tea. "How about you, Fiona, would you like another cup?"

Nodding silently, Fiona can only make herself take one breath after another and tries not to think of what might have been. Of what could be the next time such an announcement is made on the radio.

"Thank you," she says eventually, her spine straightening as the news sinks in. "I can't bear to feel happy when someone else has died, yet I can't help feeling relieved."

"That's an entirely normal response," Mrs Baines tells Fiona, as the other woman struggles to come to terms with her feelings. "But you do need to differentiate between feeling glad that your daughter isn't dead as opposed to feeling glad that someone else is. They are two entirely different things," Mrs Baines states emphatically. "We are all glad when something bad happens to someone else rather than to us or our loved ones. Yet in reality, most of us are wishing that bad things didn't have to happen at all."

Catherine is just relieved that Mrs Baines is on hand to deal with all the emotional stuff. She can barely understand her own feelings half the time, let alone comfort or reassure anyone else.

Putting her tea down, Catherine watches Fiona struggle to stay calm. "Mrs Richerson," she begins tentatively, "have you heard from your husband since the announcement on the radio?"

If possible, Fiona Richerson goes even paler than before and looks shocked by Catherine's question. "Oh my lord – Colin!"

Jesus, he must be going out of his head if he heard the news on the radio. "Ok, let's go through to the lounge and you can call him from there," Catherine tells her and guides the way through the house. "Fiona, I hope you won't take this out of turn," she begins hesitantly, "but I think you should discuss with your husband about going home. I can keep you up to date with my progress just as good via telephone...and at least you'll have each other for support."

For a moment Fiona looks torn. "Yes, yes I can see what you mean – I'm just loath to distance myself."

Catherine moves to the door to leave her in private, but hesitates to walk out of the room. "If it were my son out there, I'd need to lean on Logan just to be able to get up in the morning – you're an amazing woman, I really mean that."

When Logan arrives home he is surprised to find Catherine missing. He's already looked in his home office and in the bedroom in case she is taking a rest. Now he's starting to get just a bit concerned.

She has taken to reading in the library quite a bit lately, and he's stocked a shed-load of new books to accommodate her more academic reading tastes. Although, Catherine enjoys a good crime novel too.

Then he spots her, dressed in an ivory smock that reaches just below knee length. Logan watches as Catherine saunters along, her wavy blonde hair, now long enough to rustle with the breeze, shines with good health in the afternoon sun.

How lovely she is, and how lucky I am. But there's a sadness about her, something more than the usual troubled soul that is Catherine.

Mmm, I wonder if there's been any news about the missing kids, their mother and father must be frantic by now.

Ah, Mrs Baines has left dinner prepared – she must have nipped out, I can't hear her anywhere about.

Now look at that, a smile as bright as the sun itself and those blue eyes drinking me in like I'm the answer to a maiden's prayer. You're certainly the answer to all of mine, Catherine - the love of my life and longer if the Gods permit.

Stepping through the conservatory door and into the bright sunny garden, Logan's strong legs carry him with grace to stand before his wife.

"I've missed you today," he tells her, his voice low and full of emotion. He pulls her into arms and claims the upturned lips she offers him.

Just a kiss, just a meeting of mouths that stirs the heart and welcomes him home like nothing else.

"You taste good," Catherine smiles up at him and sighs. "If I could bottle that flavour...but no, without those incredibly soft lips to nibble on, the flavour would be meaningless."

They both chuckle and Logan steers them towards a bench near the pond and presses the plunger on the fish pellet dispenser as he passes.

Taking a seat, Logan puts an arm around her shoulders and pulls Catherine in for a hug. With his other hand, he throws the pellets into the water one at a time and they watch the fish dive after them.

"So, how was your day, dear?" Catherine asks with a comical smile and a raised brow.

"Pretty good actually," and Logan prods her in the ribs to tickle her. "I sold a project I've been developing for almost a year now. It started out as old office space and a few empty factories – now they are one big shopping mall with flats on some of the upper floors."

"Wow," Catherine sits forward to look him right in the eyes. "I didn't realise you did that kind of thing. I'm seriously impressed."

"It's a first," he tells her, with no little pride. "But...I'm thinking it will probably be my last."

Her smile falters and her brows draw together in concern. "You lost money?" she gasps, concerned only that his business might be in trouble. "Well...that's not so bad, you can have mine – it makes no difference which bank account it sits in."

Pulling her to him, Logan kisses her with gusto. "You crazy woman throwing millions away," he tells her with a hearty laugh. "But you can keep your money safe and rest easy – I made a fortune on the deal so we won't be living on the streets just yet."

Openly frowning now, Catherine shakes her head in wonder, "But I thought... So why won't you be doing it again?" she asks, now truly confused.

Throwing the last of the fish pellets into the pond, Logan brings them both to their feet.

"Let's take a walk," he suggests, and Catherine moves with him as they take a turn about the garden.

"It isn't that the project didn't go well, or that it didn't make enough money," Logan tells her thoughtfully, "but it took a lot of my time and effort, something I'm not sure I'm going to be willing to give up now that we've got the boys coming."

"Ok," Catherine tries to think things through in a logical fashion, factoring in Logan's change in circumstance. "I get that you'd want to spend time with the kids, but wouldn't you miss it?" She looks up at the mogul who is now her husband and finds herself concerned that he may become bored.

"No, not that size of project anyway," he clarifies. "It was something I'd always dreamed of doing, taking something completely dilapidated, a real blot on the landscape, and turning it into something not only functional but beautiful."

"And you did that?" Catherine smiles with pride.

"I did, but I don't feel the need to do it again," he tells her, his arm about her shoulders keeping her tight to his side. "I'm ready for family, and fatherhood and all the joys and heartaches that I know will come with it." He stops, turning Catherine to face him and looks down at her with so much love in his eyes, "I'm ready to go home...if that's still what you want?"

"To Lakelands?" she gasps, then flings her arms around his neck. "Oh, Logan...really?!"

Hugging her to him, Logan has to remind himself that she is pregnant and restrain his enthusiasm. "I've thought about it a lot since you brought up the idea," he tells her when at last he can bare to put her from him. "I won't be giving work up completely, but I've got excellent people working for me, people I can trust and I'll be able to do a lot of the managerial stuff from home."

Putting a gentle hand to his cheek, Catherine can only wonder at the good fortune that brought her this man.

Built like a warrior, she chuckles to herself. He-man and Norse God all rolled into one - a lethal combination for any woman.

Sliding her hand to the back of his head she pulls Logan down for a kiss. The heat of the kiss starts in her heart but doesn't take long to spread throughout her body with Logan's body responding in kind.

Tongues gently duel, lips taste and teeth nip, and their loins burn. Need swiftly builds and hands find pleasure in their intimate explorations.

A world of love and emotion has opened up to Catherine since Logan strode into her life. A gentle man, he is no pushover, yet if anyone can wind him around their little finger, it is she.

He loves her. He wants her. And most amazing of all, he seems to need her in his life.

"I love these dresses," he chuckles deeply as he slips the loose smock dress over her head. Then he takes a step back. "God Almighty, what a woman you are," and his brown eyes darken, feasting greedily on her perky naked breasts.

Stood in only the tiniest pair of lace panties, Catherine suddenly feels shy. "I was too hot for proper underwear," she mumbles into his heaving chest, having taken a step forward to hide her nakedness against him.

"I'm not complaining," he tells her, and runs his hands up and down her silky back, going lower each time until his large hands cup the cheeks of her bottom.

Feeling the hard length of him against her stomach, Catherine's cheeks heat but so does her passion. And passion wins out when Logan ducks his head to take her mouth, his hands moving up and around to cup her full bare breasts.

Her breath hitches as his thumb strums against her nipple and his mouth lifts from hers to take over from his thumb.

Six feet four of man-mountain is now kneeling at her feet and arousing her so profoundly that their surroundings are forgotten.

There in the bright sunshine of a summer's day, she allows him to nudge her legs apart and push his fingers inside of her.

A guttural groan rips from her throat as her head falls back and his hands wreak havoc on her body. Then his lips move down her body and her body falls, caught in his strong arms and laid gently on the ground.

When he got undressed she couldn't say, but the feel of his nakedness against her is as essential to her now as breathing.

Her hand seeks and finds him, her moan of pleasure as much a statement of possession.

Mine! Only mine...meant for me and bound to me forever.

Rolling him on to his back, Catherine moves over Logan and looks deep into his fierce eyes. She can see it there, his claim on her, his need for her and she will satisfy this man like no other woman ever has.

"I love you, Logan Sayers, and I'm going to take you inside me and ride you like a wild-woman," she tells him, her voice low and feral, and her eyes burning into him. "But first, I'm going to drive you crazy with my mouth."

He's already trembling with pleasure as her hand continues to move up and down the throbbing length of him, but when her mouth closes around him his groan is long and guttural.

His hips buck and her mouth moves with him, her tongue teases then her teeth rake the length of him. When she takes her mouth away he groans at the loss, but when she blows gently on the head of his pulsating erection he almost loses it completely.

"Jesus, Catherine." But any more words are forgotten as she takes him forcefully deep inside of her and is absolutely true to her word.

Ride him like a wild-woman is exactly what she does. Logan's hands hold onto her hips but not to restrain, more to aid her balance and rhythm.

He can feel himself tighten, can feel Catherine tightening around him and then their worlds explode and their bodies shudder, quivering together uncontrollably in the aftermath.

My woman. My heart. My life.

CHAPTER SEVEN

"Get up!" A rasping growl orders Natalie and Joshua, who are huddled together on the floor in a very cold, very dark room. "Move your fucking arses or I'll shoot you right there!"

Holding a hand up to shield his eyes from what isn't really a very bright light, Josh tries to placate their captor. "Ok. Ok. Come on Nat, I'll help you," he offers, when Natalie struggles to get to her feet.

Waving his gun at them, their captor growls out his orders, "You, stay there, and you...," he points the gun directly at Joshua, "...you come with me."

"No. N.n.no," Natalie stammers, fear and cold conspiring to steal her voice.

"It's alright, Nat. You just stay here and stay quiet…I'll be fine," Joshua reassures her, knowing that isn't the case at all.

"I said move it," the dark voice growls out impatiently. "Get your sorry arse over here!"

Placing a gentle kiss on Natalie's forehead, Joshua whispers, "Stay quiet and you'll stay alive," then he walks over to the hulking man and takes a step into the lighted corridor.

"Aahhgg…," Joshua chokes out, his breath now cut off by the monster's massive arm pulling tight across his neck and holding him against his bulk.

"Now you, girlie," the low, lascivious voice orders Natalie. But she stays rooted to the spot by fear and his dark voice booms out, "Now!"

His voice echoing throughout the vacuus building, Natalie jumps forward and darts through the door, her eyes large and round as she glimpses Joshua's purpling face.

They walk along a corridor, silent and eerie after the nights of screaming they've been forced to listen to. Natalie is scurrying but not daring to get too far ahead, afraid of what the man will do to Joshua.

But Joshua is oblivious to everything but the rush and pulse of blood in his head, his feet no longer touching the ground as the beast carries him by his neck.

"Stop! That door on the right, get inside," he booms out his orders and Natalie quickly does as she's told.

Moments later, Joshua is flung unceremoniously into the room, his body falling in a seemingly lifeless heap.

When the steel barred door clangs noisily shut, Natalie races over to Joshua and desperately tries to rouse him.

"Oh, please...please don't be dead – Josh, don't leave me...please, please, please, don't leave me," she begs him, gently shaking his shoulders, feeling for a pulse and then cradling his head in her lap when the faintest beat signals his tenuous hold on life.

"It's alright, baby, it's alright," she croons softly, rocking him gently and stroking over his hair and face with a trembling hand.

Having been kept in almost total darkness for around a week, Natalie finds herself in constant light. It never goes off; there is no night or day and even with Joshua's watch she can only tell the time, not whether it is morning or night.

It becomes impossible to estimate how long they have been missing. Will anyone really be looking for them – or will they have given up, believing them either to have run away together, or to be dead?

A whimper causes Natalie's head to snap up. It was momentary and almost inaudible, but she heard it, she's sure.

Moving to the door and looking through the steel bars, Natalie holds a hand over her mouth to stop herself from crying out.

Someone else is here, she's sure of it. There are other doors, barred the same as theirs, but she can't see anyone near them.

She, herself, is sat in a crouch about two feet away from the door itself. *What if he's out there? If he sees me at the door it might make him angry. Is that what the others think – are they terrified to be seen or heard?*

The whimper isn't repeated. The silence hangs solid and heavy and terrifying.

A sudden moan from behind her makes Natalie glad she's still got her hand over her mouth, it stifles her gasp and she returns quickly to Joshua's side.

Stroking his hair back from his face, Natalie crouches low and whispers next to his ear. "Quiet baby, you need to be quiet." But Joshua doesn't seem to hear, or just can't contain himself, and she has to put a hand over his mouth to stifle the moans. *Oh, God! If he hears us, if we attract his attention...what then?*

Suddenly, Natalie screams, along with at least one other female. A loud noise of metal against metal, like a pipe being drawn deliberately across the bars of the doors, clangs at regular intervals.

Not daring to move, hardly daring to breath, Natalie stays crouched beside Josh and just prays the monster passes them by.

Silence. It seems interminable. It feels threatening. It weighs so heavy.

Three loud clangs of metal on metal again and more than two females scream this time, but Natalie isn't one of them.

Her free hand is again clasped firmly over her mouth, her teeth biting into the soft flesh of her palm.

"You," she hears the monster shout at someone, "get your sorry arse over to this door and stay there."

"I.I didn't mean to scream," she hears a woman plead, her voice rising in pitch with every word.

His voice becomes low and menacing. "Did I give you permission to speak?" Natalie doesn't hear a reply and imagines the woman shaking her head. "And I didn't give you permission to look at me either, did I?"

Again, Natalie doesn't hear a reply. Then a different sound of metal on metal can be heard – it's the jangle of keys and then a lock being turned and finally, a door opens.

Oh please, please don't hurt her...please don't make her scream...

But scream is exactly what the woman does. Not once, and not just for a moment or two – her screams go on for hours, while everyone else prays for it to end soon and for their own deliverance.

When Emma arrives at Catherine and Logan's house, she is hyped up and ready to dive into the missing couple's case.

Grabbing her briefcase from the front seat of her trusty Skoda, Emma locks the car and heads for the house.

"You look revved," Catherine observes, watching the younger woman almost bounce from her car parked near the double garage and across the front of the house to the front door.

"I am," Emma smiles brightly and holds up her briefcase. "I have something in here you might be interested in."

"Like the next government budget," Catherine throws out with a mischievous grin, eyeing the larger than average burgundy leather briefcase that Emma is toting.

"Just wait and see," Emma grins back and strides into the house as Catherine steps aside and waves her in.

Seeing Logan coming out of the kitchen, Emma smiles and says, "Hi."

Returning her greeting, Logan smiles a welcome. "Would you like anything to drink...tea, coffee...alcohol?"

Emma gives a saucy chuckle, "Let's live dangerously and go for the latter – whatever you have is fine with me."

Catherine leads the way up to the home office that she and Logan share. They have moved a second desk in there and Catherine's laptop is already open on Logan's.

"You can use my desk," and she indicates the desk that she cleared earlier for Emma to use. "Did you bring your laptop?" she asks and eyes the burgundy briefcase with interest.

"I did," Emma smiles brightly, and stands the leather bag on the table and draws out a pristine piece of state-of-the-art computer technology.

"I thought people only put their lunches in those things," Catherine sniffs disapprovingly. She has never seen the point in pomp and briefcases have always struck her as pretentious.

"I'm sure some do, but my father gave this to me when I started university and it has served me well as a catch-all," Emma tells her easily.

"A what-all?" Catherine asks with a frown.

"A catch-all," Emma repeats with a chuckle. "Not in the strictest use of the phrase, but it fits how I've always used my briefcase. It can house my laptop," and she waves a hand at the one she has just set up on Catherine's desk, "as well as all the books and paperwork I'm likely to need in one day. It saves me having a book-bag and a computer case. Simpler...see?"

Drawing out a sheaf of papers, Emma begins to set a few of them out across the desk.

Not able to argue with her logic, Catherine begins to read what Emma has brought with her.

"You've been busy," she comments, nodding and moving from page to printed page. "You've found a few of the same cases as me," and Catherine points to the pages that detail the murders Emma has deemed to be similar in some way to the disappearance of Natalie and Joshua.

Having picked one up, Catherine is studying the details as she paces the room.

"White wine ok?" Logan asks a moment later, and watches Emma nod and smile in appreciation as he hands her a glass.

Knowing better than to disturb Catherine when she is deep in thought, Logan puts her smaller glass of wine on his own desk and takes a sip of the one he is left holding.

Stopping, Catherine turns and frowns over at Emma. "What made you list the Watson and Carver cases – their disappearances were never connected and they weren't thought to have been courting for long before they went missing?"

"True," Emma takes a sip of her wine and crosses the room to Catherine. "But look at the circumstances. They were both known to enjoy country walks, lived near a national park that has a similar environment to Matlock and both disappeared around the same time."

"That was never proven," Catherine persists. "I looked at this one; she was definitely known to have gone missing within a twenty-four hour time frame – he could have disappeared anytime in the preceding week. He lived alone and didn't work so no one could pinpoint his last known whereabouts." Shaking her head, Catherine reaches absently for the wine Logan had provided and stands contemplating the research before her.

"See...here," and Catherine holds the sheet out for Emma to read and, with a finger unfurled from her wine glass, points to a paragraph of particular interest. "It says he was thought to have moved on to find work."

"It also says that he appeared to have left all his belongings behind," Emma persists, standing her ground. "Even though they were meagre and not of any great value, how many people do you know who would just up sticks and walk out without saying goodbye to even one person?"

Logan stands by the door watching the exchange and wonders whether to duck for cover or brave it and stay to referee. "Perhaps you just need a 'maybe' pile," he suggests, then holds up a hand and decides to duck and run when two pairs of combative eyes turn and scorch him. "Or not. I'll be in the library if you need me," he smiles, and pulls the office door closed behind him.

The two women look at each other and, seeing the other's frown of annoyance, smile then give a chuckle of understanding.

"Guess we scared him off." Emma looks to the closed door then back at Catherine.

"Good," Catherine smiles easily, "he's too damned distracting anyway."

Emma lifts her brow at the implication of Catherine's words, and Catherine blushes wildly when she realises just what she's said.

"Well he is," Catherine snarls, embarrassment causing her to snap.

"I agree," Emma holds her hands up in surrender, and then tries to backtrack when Catherine's top lip turns up in a snarl. "In a totally non-threatening, I promise not to touch, kind of a way."

Then, when Catherine continues to give her the evil eye, Emma snaps and stands with her hands on her hips facing her down with an exasperated frown. "Jesus, Catherine, get over it! You married a prime male whose drop-dead-gorgeous looks and sexy body would cause any woman with a pulse to salivate. You just have the good fortune to know that he only has eyes for you!"

Catherine's snarl gradually fades and her lips instead pull into a smug smile. "Huh, who knew!"

Rolling her eyes, Emma gives the sheet of paper Catherine is still holding a flick with her finger. "So, back to the case — are we going to put this one on a 'maybe' pile as Logan suggested?"

Frowning again, Catherine eyes the page unconvinced but says, "If it'll keep you quiet, yes, though I don't expect anything to come of it."

The two women work well together, reviewing the cases they've already found and looking for others to add to their steadily growing list.

"Hell, Catherine, if even half of these cases are attributable to our perp', he's a prolific murderer and has possibly been operating over the last fifteen years," Emma states with an incredulous and heartfelt sigh as she leans back in her seat.

Looking up from her laptop, Catherine nods in agreement. "These can't all be coincidental abductions, and you're right, he's been a busy boy. That's why I'm going to give Inspector Harper a call – I'm not convinced that anyone has put all these cases together."

"Inspector Harper?" Emma's brows draw together quizzically.

"He's the cop who was originally on my mother's murder case," Catherine explains. "I worked with him to help finally catch the murdering SOB."

"Ah, yes, I read the article," Emma tells her. "So, is this what you did to help?" and she waves a hand at their computers.

"Pretty much," Catherine confirms. "Though I had the luck, if that's what you can call it, to overhear a conversation Logan was having with the murderer's father – his voice was distinctive and almost identical to the one I'd remembered hearing as a child."

Her thoughts drift back to the awful memory of her mother's murder. 'Just look what this one can do', and Catherine can hear the vile monster's Welsh voice sniggering in her head as he held up one of his instruments of torture for her to see before using it to brutally mutilate her mother.

Then she registers Emma's gasp and realises her mistake.

"You were there...?" Emma asks quietly, and with undisguised compassion.

Straightening her spine, Catherine becomes angry. "That snippet of gossip isn't for public consumption," she glares over at Emma. "Only a very few people know that I was forced to watch what that low-life did to my mother and now you're one of them – don't go spreading it around!"

Not having the heart to be affronted, Emma only shakes her head. "Of course not Catherine, I would never betray your trust."

Walking into the library to find Logan, Catherine looks tired and worn out.

"I was just about to come up and call a halt," he tells her as Catherine crosses the room towards him. "Is Emma still here?"

"No, she went about half an hour ago." Catherine yawns and plops herself on his knees.

"You're so warm and safe," she tells him, and snuggles into his wonderfully broad chest and enjoys the feel of his strong arms cradling her against him.

"I'll keep you safe, Catherine," he croons against her hair, his deep voice rumbling softly over her jagged nerves and calming them instantly. "I won't let anyone hurt you, ever again."

"You can't protect me from the world, Logan," she sighs and snuggles in deeper. "There are some pretty sick people out there and I have to find this particular one as fast as I can."

"Find him, or find the missing couple, Catherine?" he asks with growing concern.

"Doesn't it amount to the same thing?" Lifting her head, Catherine kisses the pulse in his neck and it jumps beneath her lips. Continuing her assault on his senses, she hopes to distract him.

"You know it doesn't," Logan breathes out with growing difficulty as Catherine's hand is now gliding over his chest having popped a couple of buttons on his shirt and slipped it inside.

Her voice becomes sultry as she asks him, "Take me to bed, Logan, I want to forget what I've seen tonight."

Dropping his lips to cover hers, Logan soon transports her thoughts out of the realms of torture and death and fills them instead with sensation and need.

He's aware of what she's doing, of course. Not only does she want to forget for a while, but she's trying to distract him from that all important question.

If she's trying to trace the missing couple, then fine. If she's trying to track down and capture a potential killer, that is far from fine! And he determines to find out which it is over breakfast in the morning.

For tonight he'll give Catherine what she needs, and enjoy doing so. Pregnant with their boys, she still pulls at the core of him. He wants her no less now that she has grown round and full and even loves her new shape and the swell of her breasts.

His wife. Soon to be the mother of his children. Those thoughts still amaze and bring him untold joy every day.

What a woman you are! What a huge heart you have! But you scare me, Catherine, with all that courage and determination to fight for the suffering. It causes you pain and I feel it too. I just want to keep you safe. Keep you with me. Love you always.

CHAPTER EIGHT

Mrs Baines is busy cooking breakfast when Catherine saunters into the kitchen giving a huge yawn.

"Aren't you sleeping well?" the housekeeper asks Catherine with a motherly look of concern.

But Catherine chuckles light-heartedly. "I slept like a log; I just seem to take longer to come round these days."

"Well that's good to hear," Mrs Baines smiles and nods approvingly. "Would you like bacon with your scrambled eggs this morning?"

Pursing her lips in consideration, Catherine unconsciously rubs her belly, "You know, that sounds great!" And the two women beam at each other.

"There's some freshly squeezed orange juice on the table, just give me a minute and I'll bring your breakfast through."

Logan is already seated in the conservatory. He folds the newspaper he's reading and greets her with an adoring smile.

"You going into the office today?" she asks, then watches as Logan shakes his head.

"No, I have plenty of work that I can do from home. You?"

No, she hadn't been planning to go into the office, but she didn't relish trying to continue what she and Emma had gotten into last night with Logan looking over her shoulder.

As if hearing her turmoil in the silence, Logan nods and stirs his tea.

"It isn't like I'll be going after the monster myself," Catherine tells him, interpreting Logan's contemplation of his tea stirring correctly.

"But you are going after him?" he tries to clarify, already knowing the answer.

Silently, Catherine nods, then smiles up at Mrs Baines, grateful for her interruption of their reluctant conversation.

As the woman places a plate of scrambled eggs on toast with bacon on the side in front of Catherine, she thanks the woman then asks her, "Do you have any children, Mrs Baines?"

Taken a little aback, the housekeeper gives Catherine a considering frown. Her employers didn't usually ask such personal questions, though she had no objection to answering. "We weren't that lucky, my Larry and me. I suppose that's a lot to do with why I chose to work with children." When Catherine doesn't explain her question, Mrs Baines asks, "What made you ask?"

Blushing and looking at Logan under her lashes, Catherine isn't sure how to go about asking for this kindly woman's help.

A hand on her ever expanding stomach, Catherine eventually says, "It won't be long till we have two, and I don't know the first thing about being a mother." Her cheeks redden further, "I was hoping you might consider extending your role to include me and the children?"

Mrs Baines is so taken aback that she pulls out a chair and sits without being asked. "Well, that's a bolt from the blue and no mistake," and she looks wide eyed from Catherine to Logan. Then realising her bad manners jumps up from her seat apologising.

But Logan waves her back down, smiling at this homely woman's discomfort at having crossed over some imaginary employer/employee line.

He hasn't thought of her like that in a long time. Not since she helped Catherine after the night they'd confronted and helped to capture Charlie Edwards, her mother's murderer.

She'd been a gem then and many times since. She really is just like family.

"I hadn't realised you were thinking along those lines," Logan reaches over to give Catherine's hand a squeeze of reassurance. "But I think it's a marvellous idea. Were you thinking about Lakelands too?" he asks quietly.

Catherine nods and bites her bottom lip. Turning to the bemused housekeeper, she expands on her idea. "You know that Logan's father still lives in their large house in the Shires," Catherine begins then continues at Mrs Baines' nod. "Well, he's all alone there – apart from Aida who comes in a few times a week to help out. And we were thinking of moving in – permanently," she adds at the housekeeper's quizzical frown.

"Is it far – I mean, would you want me to commute?"

"Err, no, not really," Catherine answers, then looks up at Logan in a silent plea for help.

"I think what Catherine is trying to ask you," Logan begins cautiously, "is whether or not you might consider moving to Lakelands with us – making it your home too?"

Mrs Baines' eyes go wide in astonishment. It isn't like she has anything holding her in Sheriton, but what about her little cottage – would she really want to give that up?

Pre-empting what he fears may be a reflexive no, Logan continues, "Lakelands is a huge estate, and it has beautiful grounds, the lake it is named after, and a house that can easily provide you with your own private accommodations. And I could help you to rent out your current home, if that is what you decide you'd like to do."

Blowing out a long breath, the housekeeper tries to take it all in. "Is this move to Lakelands definite?" she asks. And when they both nod, she takes a moment to think, "Well, I don't want to lose either of you – I enjoy my work and the people I work for." For just a second or two she hesitates then smiles brightly, "If you're going then so am I, and I'd be delighted to add you and the children into my duties. In fact, it would be my pleasure."

Giving a huge sigh of relief, Catherine beams at Mrs Baines and then at Logan. "Well, now I can start looking forward to the boys' arrival. I've been terrified at the thought of how I'll manage when they do make an appearance."

"You should have said, I'd have tried to solve the problem sooner," Logan chides her gently.

"Well, now it's solved and the two of you can go ahead with your arrangement," Mrs Baines smile delightedly. "And I'd appreciate your help with renting the cottage, thank you."

Getting to her feet, the housekeeper returns to her chores with a spring in her step.

"It's really going to happen," Catherine turns to Logan in wonder. "We'd better go down there soon to discuss the move with your dad – check he's still up for the idea."

"That won't be a problem, but I do think a visit is in order," Logan tells her, a contented smile making his brown eyes warm and soft.

They work together in Logan's home office for the first half of the morning. But when Catherine decides it's time to telephone Inspector Harper, to give him an overview of what she and Emma have found and ask him for his input, she goes down to the lounge to make the call.

"There are so many similarities," Catherine tells the inspector, "it just defies logic to think that none of them are connected."

"Hmm, I have to agree," the inspector's deep voice growls in contemplation. "If you wouldn't mind, I'd like to pay you a visit with a colleague of mine, Detective Sloane Shivers. We could come over this afternoon, if that's convenient?"

"Shivers?" Catherine asks dubiously. "Really?"

The inspector gives a chuckle, "How does three-thirty sound?"

"If you can make it four-thirty I can have Emma here to join us?" she says, then smiles at his confirmation. "It's just that, Emma has worked as hard as I have on this and she has her own views on some of them."

"That's fine then, we'll see you this afternoon." Then the inspector is gone and Catherine is left contemplating the meeting.

Going back up to her office, she rings Emma to ask if she can come over for the meeting. "It's not a problem if you have something else on," Catherine assures Emma, "I just told them that I'd like you to be able to give your own opinions as we differ on some of the cases we found."

Confirming that she would be there, Emma also accepts Catherine's offer to stay to dinner afterwards.

"That sounds interesting," Logan observes when Catherine sits back in her chair. "Do you mind if I sit in?"

Brows raised Catherine eyes her husband warily. "Why – I didn't think you approved of me doing this?"

Sighing heavily, Logan gets to his feet then sits on the edge of Catherine's desk looking down at her. "I don't approve or disapprove," he tells her. "I'm just concerned about the effect such an emotional and time-consuming project might have on you and the boys."

Reaching out, Logan cups her cheek. "I couldn't be more proud of what you're trying to do. That you care enough to take the trouble." His thumb traces her full lower lip. "I just wish it didn't hurt you on such a personal level."

"I'm..."

"No..." his thumb moves to stop her from uttering the lie, "...don't tell me that you're fine. I've been watching you go through those cases that you and Emma identified and it hurts you. The pain and suffering of the victims and their families...it hurts you deeply."

Unable to deny it, unable to tell him a bare faced lie, Catherine finally nods. "Ok, so it hurts me – but not half as much as doing nothing would." Her round blue eyes plead for understanding. "Now that I know, now that we've uncovered so many possibilities, how can I walk away? It just wouldn't be right," she tells him, and watches Logan nod in understanding.

"Then let me help," he suggests, stunning her into silence. "We worked well together before – let me share the workload and the emotional burden!"

Standing, Catherine winds her arms about his neck and moves to kiss the side of his neck. "You are the kindest, most caring husband a woman could ask for." Tightening her hold briefly, she moves her lips over his jaw-line and gradually takes his lips with hers.

Opening his knees, Logan pulls her closer, deepening the kiss when Catherine tangles her fingers in his hair.

He has never wanted a woman the way he wants Catherine. His body is always quick to respond to her slightest encouragement, and even without it he can't get enough of her.

Her mind is unravelling. Her body responding in a way that makes her feel wanton. Ever since this wonderful man showed her the beauty of physical love, she has burned for him in a way she would have thought impossible.

Her introduction to the opposite sex had been brutal and terrifying. Nothing could have surprised her more than when she had responded so wholeheartedly to Logan's ministrations.

It makes her smile even to think of the first time Logan had touched her so intimately. She had fainted, of all things. Climaxed so profoundly that it had quite literally blown her mind and the lights had gone out instantly.

He had teased her, of course, but Logan had reassured her too. The next time had been different and she had been determined. He had taken her up with his expert hands and when she had climaxed he'd backed off, not wanting to take her virginity. But she had had other ideas and had surprised him, thrown him onto his back and impaled herself upon him, thus taking the decision about her virginity out of his hands.

Now they love easily and they always love well. Logan knows how to please her, and Catherine opens to him willingly. She can enjoy his caresses, can even laugh when he teases her, and always wants more. So much more.

One large hand cups her breast, her tender nipple stiffening quickly. Catherine feels his other hand cup her bottom, pulling her against his groin, making her fully aware of his growing need of her.

Sliding her hand down between them, she feels along the hard length of him and also feels her panties become instantly wet. *Christ I want you! I always want you! It's just never enough!*

His lips trail up her neck, nibbling on her earlobe then his tongue sends unimaginable thrills through her body when it licks and probes before his dark voice says, "I think this would be the perfect time to take a rest on the bed."

She can feel his hot breath in her ear and draws back to raise an eyebrow, "Rest? That's not exactly what I have in mind."

He chuckles and bites gently on her earlobe, "I meant after. A bit of sexercise is good for you; it'll make you relax that much more."

Giggling at his extremely suggestive tone, Catherine allows him to sweep her up into his lovely strong arms and carry her off to the nearby bedroom.

He was right, Catherine yawns three hours later, *sex really is a good relaxant.*

She is alone in their bed now. Logan, having fallen asleep with Catherine while he held her after their 'sexercise', has gotten up and is now going through hers and Emma's findings.

Having pulled her underwear and a robe on, Catherine stands leaning on the door-jam watching him. "He's prolific...and he's been doing it for a long, long time."

"I agree." Logan frowns darkly as he reads about one abduction after another, one dead body after another and the tortures each suffered, prior to the release of their deaths.

"I've been so selfish," Logan moans softly. "Not wanting you to get involved – but this is pure evil. It needs to be stopped!"

Moving into the room, Catherine puts her arm through his and leans into his solid frame, stiff and tense with realisation. "You haven't got a selfish bone in your body," she tells him, and turns to kiss his arm.

"I want to help with this," Logan looks down at her with serious eyes. "I want to wring this perverts neck and I want to bring Natalie and Joshua home before he does this to them."

Moving to stand in front of him, Catherine looks up at Logan and puts a hand to his cheek. "I want that too, but we need to keep this real."

"What does that mean?" Logan frowns down at her.

"It means, we have to accept that that may not be possible," then when he makes to protest, Catherine uses her thumb on his lips to still them. "We'll try, Logan. All of us; you, me and Emma and Inspector Harper and his cronies, we'll all try our best – but we need to accept that we may fail to bring them home safe. Though not getting our hands on that bas...I mean, that pervert is not an option. We keep going until we find him!"

Too damn right!

CHAPTER NINE

By the time Inspector Harper arrives for their meeting, Emma and Catherine have blue-tacked all the information to a wall in chronological order of disappearance, with another section for the order of the eventual discovery of their bodies.

It isn't a pretty sight — they have pictures as well as graphic details pinned up, and it makes for the stuff of horror movies.

Logan has finished up his business for the day and is helping the girls to prepare. When the inspector arrives with Detective Shivers, he goes down to escort them to his office.

"Ladies, Inspector Harper and Detective Shivers have arrived," Logan announces, and smiles at Emma's obvious attraction to the younger man at his side.

"Oh...my...lord," Emma groans so that only Catherine can hear, "he makes me shiver just looking at him."

Giving her an elbow in the ribs, Catherine moves forward with a smile and a hand held out to Inspector Harper, "Nice to see you again Inspector."

Returning her smile, Inspector Harper shakes her outstretched hand then gives a wave at his colleague. "I think we can get on a first name basis in the privacy of your home." The inspector's smile widens. "Just call me Frank, and this is Sloane," and he jerks his head to indicate the man at his side.

"Hi." The greeting is more of a moan as Emma moves forward and holds her hand out to Sloane, "I'm Emma."

Her brown eyes have all but melted as she takes in the detective's terrific body, gorgeous hair and knock out good looks.

"Sloane," he states, taking her hand in a firm grip, then letting it go like he's just been scolded. "Pleased to meet you."

"Shall we get started," Logan invites, trying to keep a straight face. He remembers feeling a jolt of electricity up his own arm the moment he'd taken Catherine's hand for the first time — and if he isn't mistaken, Sloane was experiencing the same response to Emma.

"Absolutely," Frank Harper agrees, and moves further into the room. "Impressive," he nods, his hand rubbing over his chin as he looks over the work they have pinned up on the wall. "Good God, this is amazing!" His head is shaking in wonder, his eyes wide with shock, "I don't know of anyone whose put all this together – you put us to shame," he looks from Catherine to Emma and nods his head sagely.

Sloane Shivers moves forward to inspect the printouts more closely. "Are these police records – how did you..."

But he doesn't get to finish that thought as Frank Harper gives him an elbow in the ribs.

However, it's Catherine who speaks out first. "Are we going to have a problem with you, Shivers?" she asks, deliberately using his last name. "Because if we are, you can leave right now!"

The room falls silent and all eyes turn to the detective.

Sloane looks to Inspector Harper and assesses the situation. "If Frank doesn't have a problem then neither do I." Then he smiles over at Catherine, a gleam of admiration in his eyes now.

"That's what I thought," Catherine tells him, her rigid stance easing as she makes to take them through what she and Emma have found.

"There doesn't appear to be a pattern, unless you think the randomness of the abductions is a pattern in itself," she explains. "The abduction sites range all over the country and may even spread out over the entire British Isles – we just haven't had time to search that far."

"Christ all bloody mighty," Sloane frowns, looking at a map detailing all the suspected connected cases. "If this is correct, we could be looking at one of the most prolific serial killers of all time – and spanning decades," his frown deepens and suddenly Catherine's computer crimes seem utterly insignificant.

Nodding, Catherine agrees, "Precisely. There are some cases where the modus-operandi is so strikingly similar that it beggars belief to think that any two people would commit the same crime in exactly the same way."

"That's what we call a perp's MO," Sloane explains. "And perp' stands for..."

"Perpetrator, as in the person who carried out the crime," Catherine finishes for him with an eyebrow raised. "We girlies actually managed to figure that one out for ourselves," she tells him, and then laughs at his reddening cheeks.

"Ok, so, now that we've established the basics, let's get back to it. Although we have some cases that are, as I said, strikingly similar, we also have a few that are borderline," and Catherine turns to Emma to take up the brief.

"I have found some abductions where the male and female are thought to have been taken separately and probably not even on the same day," Emma begins. Then, as she draws breath to continue, Sloane interrupts.

"Then how are they connected to the couples killer?"

Catherine frowns, "The couples killer — is that what the police are calling him?"

"I have no idea," Sloane tells her, "but it seems obvious that that is what he's doing." Then he hesitates and moves to look at the map again, "Or it could be what 'they' are doing," and puts a lot of emphasis on 'they'.

Moving to stand beside him, Catherine considers that thought. "That's a possibility, though not probable," she turns to Sloane. "It would take an awful lot of trust or intimidation for someone to rope a second person in as their partner, or assistant. I mean, how would he scope a possible candidate out — you couldn't just walk up to an ordinary Joe Bloggs and expect him to commit murder?"

"And do the horrific things that some of these victims have had done to them," Emma adds, pointing to the photographs.

"That's true, you're both absolutely right," Sloane agrees, his stance unchanged, "but it certainly wouldn't be the first time it's happened. These people seem to sniff out their own – it's like paedophiles, they gravitate towards each other, have their own like-minded communities."

Emma grimaces and can't help cringing back a step, "Just the thought of that is enough to turn my stomach. What we're dealing with is bad enough, but kids..." And Emma lets the thought hang in the air.

"Christ!" Logan groans and moves to his desk to pick up the telephone. Calling down to the kitchen, he asks Mrs Baines to bring up a tray of tea and coffee with a few biscuits if they have any. Then he moves back to what is becoming a lively discussion.

"I didn't say they were an exact match," Emma fights her corner, "but they do have enough common factors to keep them on the wall and to be considered part of this investigation!"

Catherine is frowning heavily, "We've got enough cases without adding rank outsiders – and we haven't even looked at the rest of the British Isles," she adds ominously. "Christ knows how many we'll have when we get around to looking at those!"

"You wouldn't say that if it were one of your boys out there – we can't just dismiss those," Emma points at the outlying group. "We need to stand for them all until we get proof to the contrary."

Giving a reluctant nod, Catherine concedes. "Alright, we keep them in...for now," she adds, but Emma is satisfied and continues to go through each case and it's common factors for the others in the group.

"I have to agree with Emma," Sloane nods, his expression wrapped in concentration. "I know these aren't as clear cut as the rest, but there's enough there to warrant further investigation."

They look at the time lines, first the abductions and then the discovery of the bodies.

"There's no crossover," Frank Harper observes, "no reason to suspect two killers – other than the amount of victims," he adds.

"Exactly," Catherine nods in agreement. "Although it would mean one person covering a lot of miles, they are all possibly the work of one organised mind."

"What makes you say that?" Logan asks, having rejoined the group.

"What?" Catherine looks over to him confused.

"That he has an organised mind. Couldn't it just be that he's following the route required of his job?" Logan asks. "Like a rep' or a lorry driver, someone who has a reason to be in all those places at those particular times."

Again Catherine nods, but points to the list of recovered bodies. "I think that's entirely possible, even probable," she agrees, "but I also think he's a dab hand at planning. Just look at the sites where the victims were found – most have been returned to within five miles of their original abduction site. Considering the amount of victims, it follows that he must be organised, even compulsive to some extent, as he risks being discovered by returning to the scenes of the crimes."

Frank Harper nods and squints to take a more detailed look at the discovery dates. "Have you tried to find a pattern in the amount of time between the abduction and finding the victims?"

Catherine looks at Emma and the younger woman shrugs. "No, it appears that neither of us thought of that angle."

Sloane nods sagely, "You're not trained to think of all the angles," he tells the girls, trying to sooth away any disappointment. "But we are, that's why it will be good to work together on this."

Feeling out of sorts for not taking the logical next step, Catherine quickly grabs paper and a pen and does the calculations. In minutes she has all the information that Sloane could want, and a bit more.

"It seems we have a six weeks pattern – though there are exceptions." Catherine moves to the wall and pins up two lists. "These all fall into the six week pattern almost exactly," she points to one list then points to the other. "But these are either twelve weeks or haven't yet been found."

Frowning deeply, his handsome face grimacing at an unpleasant thought, Sloane sighs, "So, he might still have the poor bastards!"

"God Almighty!" Frank blows out a whoosh of breath and pulls a handkerchief out of his pocket to wipe his brow.

It doesn't even occur to Catherine to admonish Sloane for swearing in front of her unborn children; both she and Emma are trying not to feel the emotions of the case they are trying to solve. If they do, they know it will only make the job harder, if not impossible to do.

"Ok," Logan breaks the deep silence, "if we assume that these cases are related, then he must be holding them somewhere. How many abductees have yet to be found?"

All eyes turn to Catherine's lists and it is plain to everyone that the number is into double figures.

"I make it thirteen," Logan continues when no one else takes up the thread he's pulling on. "That's quite a number of people, at least half of whom are men, to house and keep under control."

"And feed," Catherine adds, "if he wants to keep them healthy enough for his purpose." Then she turns to Logan's desk and her open laptop. "He needs somewhere isolated; those injuries would have caused a lot of pain and screams would be heard in the middle of an estate," she clarifies when Emma frowns. "And if he's keeping them for three months and more, they might become ill – maybe he's medicating them to prevent that, or at least ward it off," she tells anyone whose listening.

Her fingers are flying over the keyboard and everyone watches in wonder at her intense and concentrated efforts. "Got it! Tazocin!"

Sending a printout to the printer, Catherine jumps up and rounds the desk. It only takes a second or two but Catherine is bouncing on her toes.

"At least four of the victims were found to have antibiotics in their system – likely the broad-spectrum antibiotic known as Tazocin," Catherine states and pins the information to the wall next to all the other information they have gathered.

When no one looks as excited as she feels, Catherine frowns and snaps, "What? Why aren't you all doing a happy dance – we just need to trace a supplier, or look at doctors who might have a reason to travel in the same circles as our victims."

Emma decides to brave Catherine's wrath, as all the men seem reluctant to do so. "That's only four out of a possible fifteen discovered victims that we know of – it hardly forms a pattern, they could have had illnesses that required antibiotics just prior to being abducted."

Seeing the male section of her small audience nod in agreement, Catherine puts her hands on her hips and her swollen belly protrudes even more markedly. "Jesus! What a bunch of doubters!" Returning to her computer she reads off some statistics concerning the drug. "The half-life of Tazocin, that's how long it stays in the system," she explains, "is less than a day in most normally functioning humans. Even if they have some kidney or liver disorder, it still wouldn't be in the system after a week, let alone six!"

"So, if it was found in the victim's blood work, it had to have been administered after they were taken," Emma summarises, and smiles over at Catherine.

"Exactly!" Catherine gets up and points once again to the lists she pinned up. "These victims were autopsied by the same Medical Examiner, it could be that the others had different tests that simply didn't show the drug to be in the system – but that doesn't mean that it wasn't there!"

Sloane looks at Catherine, a frown forming over his grey eyes. "And you just found that all out, just now – you just tapped into your computer and found the ME reports on all the victims?"

A long, heavy silence falls over the room which Catherine eventually breaks. "Does it matter?" Her tone is defiant and her chin has gone up. "I just found a clue that could help track down this monster and put him away – your scruples won't save victims lives!"

Even Emma, who has been imagining Sloane with his clothes off and in her bed for the last hour or more, turns on Sloane with her razor sharp tongue. "Get off the moral high-ground and take a look at these people!" Her hand whips out to point at the photographs of the victims' bodies and to the photographs of them in happier times, before they were taken. "That could be your niece or nephew, your aunt or uncle, even your parents," and she points to the one couple who were in their mid-fifties when they were abducted.

"These people," she put a lot of emphasis on the word, "are not just victims – that's too impersonal a word for who they were. And if we can get the bastard that took them from their families by skirting the law, then I for one am all for it!"

Catherine is stood with her hands clamped on either side of her belly, once again shielding her babies' ears from the profanities that are flying around.

"The law is there for a reason," Sloane replies, not moving when Emma steps forward to stand right in his face. "I'm not saying that Catherine would use whatever information she is able to access for anything other than a good cause – but there are people out there who would have a field day with what she can do!"

Her eyes, hard as diamonds, look into Sloane's, "She doesn't work for 'them', never has and never will, so your point is moot!"

Getting angry now, Sloane moves to stand toe-to-toe with Emma, "My point is the law can't be ridden over rough-shod and..."

Frank Harper claps a hand on the younger man's shoulder and puts a stop to the argument. "I warned you that things might not be entirely above board – you said you could handle that. Was I wrong to bring you in on this?"

Seconds tick by loudly as Sloane Shivers contemplates his choices. "No!" he finally concedes, and takes a step back from a still glaring Emma. "No, I'm in."

"Down girl," Catherine moves to Emma's side and puts a hand on her arm. "Then let's get back to work and see what other connections we can make!"

The screaming has finally stopped and Joshua has regained consciousness. Natalie is so relieved that he appears to be none-the-worse after being almost choked to death by the brute holding them prisoner.

Describing what had just happened, the appearance of their captor and what he'd done to one poor woman, Natalie cries silent tears and trembles with fear.

"He'll come for me," she tells Josh, her tears falling like rain down dirty cheeks, "it's just a matter of time."

Putting an arm around her shoulders, Joshua tries to give comfort but finds her prediction hard to argue with. "You said she screamed first, then looked him in the eyes and spoke without his permission," Joshua summarises thoughtfully. "Maybe that's his trigger...maybe he's some sort of control freak who plays by his own sick rules. If you make sure you don't ever scream, look him in the eyes or speak without his permission, then you might go unnoticed, or at least unharmed."

It is wishful thinking for the most part, but he has little else in the way of comfort to offer Natalie. And if it eases her fear even a little, then wishful thinking will do just fine.

At some point a tray is slipped into a box that has an opening into their room and an opening that is always locked in the corridor.

It is always the same, cold soup and a drink that tastes bitter. But they eat and drink it anyway; it is all they have and all they are likely to get.

At first, they had left the tray in the box and not touched the contents. But in the end, after the same tray had stayed there for what they guessed were a couple of days, they had eaten and drunk the meagre offering and the tray had finally been taken away.

Since then, it has been replaced regularly with the same dish-water soup and disgusting drink. But Joshua told Natalie that they had to survive and starving themselves wouldn't aid their cause.

"Seven o'clock," Joshua notes at the sound of the tray being replaced, "it's like clockwork."

"Maybe we can use that to tell how many days are passing?" Natalie suggests.

Looking brighter, Joshua smiles and nods, "You're right, let's try to remember how many trays we've already had then continue to count as we get new ones."

"We won't know if it's night or morning, but at least we'll know how many days are passing," Natalie smiles, then it fades as another thought dawns. "The more day's we're here the less likely it is that anyone will still be looking for us – I'm not sure I want to count them after-all."

But Josh decides that he will, he just won't tell Nat if that's what she prefers. To him, even a little knowledge is better than nothing at all, and he determines to start taking note of any sounds that might give a clue to where they are being held.

One day they will get out of there, he has to believe that, and then they will need to be able to tell the police as much as possible for them to catch the monster.

The monster is how they both think of the man who is holding them. They know he is larger and stronger than any man they've ever known, and he is sadistic beyond belief.

When he takes one of the women into the centre of the large room and ties her to the table there, he always forces the woman's partner to witness what he does to her. The man goes wild, shouting curses and pleading for mercy, then swears to kill him when he gets his hands on him. But the monster just laughs and rapes and brutalises the women until they are too exhausted to scream any more or just pass out cold.

Natalie sits with her hand over her mouth for most of the time, sealing in any scream she might utter, that might get her noticed by the monster.

CHAPTER TEN

Speaking to Fiona Richerson is painful and not something Catherine relishes.

She tries to keep the woman up to date with their progress without raising her hopes or plunging her into a depression – but it is getting harder as the days pass.

When she walks into the conservatory for breakfast after one such talk with Fiona, it is plain for all to see that it had been a particularly difficult conversation.

"You look pale, Catherine," Logan observes kindly. "Perhaps you should take a rest this morning; we could go and visit with your sisters?"

Shaking her head Catherine pours herself a glass of orange juice. "I just talked to the mother of a daughter who may, as we speak, be being raped, tortured, or worse, murdered! And you want me to go talk babies and drink tea with my sisters..."

Her words hurt him, but Logan knew better than to take offence. Catherine is hurting too, she's hurting so badly that she isn't sleeping properly and is losing her appetite – both things he had feared when she took on this impossible task.

"I want you to clear your head for a while," he tells her softly. "I want you to give yourself time to feel normal and loved – you're bogged down in the worst kind of horrors that man can inflict on his fellow man and it's making you ill."

"It'll still be there when I get back to it, only Natalie and Joshua may be a little nearer the end – I can't walk away, Logan, I just can't," she tells him, and pushes the plate of scrambled eggs that Mrs Baines has placed in front of her away.

On seeing her do so, Logan actually becomes angry, a side of Logan that Catherine rarely sees. "We're going, and you had better pull that plate back in front of you and start eating if you want me to ever let you get back on the case again!" When Catherine's head shoots up and her blue eyes flash fire at him, Logan only glares right back. "Eat, Catherine, or I swear I'll tear down every piece of paper in that office and burn the damned lot! And I'm not averse to smashing that bloody laptop of yours either!"

"You wouldn't dare!"

"Eat, Catherine, or we'll soon see just what I do dare!"

Still glaring, and angry as the demons of hell, Catherine pulls her plate back and starts to eat. Only when he can see that she intends to continue eating does Logan continue with his own meal.

Minutes pass in stony silence, then the storm passes and the atmosphere eases. "I spoke to my father this morning," Logan tells her, and notices a reluctant interest from Catherine and smiles. "He sends his love and wants us to visit soon."

Looking up, Catherine wants to ask whether he's talked about them moving to Lakeland, but feels reluctant to give in, so turns back to her breakfast with a frown.

Logan's smile widens, he can see she's dying to ask but is just too stubborn. He considers keeping her in suspense as punishment but can't bear to see her unhappy.

"He wants to talk to us about moving in," he tells her casually, then laughs when her eyes brighten and a smile that she can't quite hide tugs at her lips. "You are one stubborn woman," he laughs and finally drags a full smile from Catherine.

"Well, you made me mad," she grumbles childishly. Then she beams a smile that makes his heart clench, "Is he really pleased about the idea?"

"He's overjoyed," Logan tells her. "Apparently you read the situation absolutely right, he admitted that he's been hoping for just this to happen ever since I first met you. It seems he knew you were the one for me right off the bat and his hopes grew from there."

Nodding, Catherine remembers her first visit to Lakelands, her conversations with Henry and finding him going through a large book of blueprints for the house to see how he could modernise it. And all to tempt his son back home.

"Your dad is one in a million," she smiles over at Logan. "He'd do anything to get you back home."

"Anything but come right out and ask," Logan frowns into his coffee. "You two should get along just fine, you've both got a stubborn streak a mile wide!"

Having finished breakfast, they say goodbye to Mrs Baines, who is thrilled to see that Catherine actually ate a full meal for once, then head off to see Adrianne.

During the short drive, Logan can't help wondering about Fiona Richerson; something had happened to put Catherine off her breakfast and she had looked pale when she'd come into the conservatory. But he is loath to bring up the topic of the missing kids again – Catherine already feels guilty about taking some time out for herself and he decides to leave it alone.

Adrianne must have spotted them coming down the long drive to the house as she is bouncing on the steps when they get out of the car.

Immediately flinging her arms about her sister, Adrianne pulls her in for a huge hug. "I've missed you. It always seems like ages in between visits, but now I'll be able to visit you," she laughs and drags them in through the large oak door.

Laughing with her, and enjoying seeing Adrianne looking better than she has in a long while, Catherine takes the seat that she and Logan are shown to in the lounge.

"So I take it the sickness has finally gone?" Catherine smiles up at Adrianne, who seems to have too much pent up energy to sit.

"Oh, it has, it has." And she beams so much, her brilliant blue Irish eyes gleam with happiness. "I've actually been out to visit with Caroline, we just went to the park together and for a short walk, but it was exhilarating not to feel ill."

"I'll bet – is Robert at work?" Catherine enquires.

"He's really busy at the moment, the business seems to be growing so fast," she tells them, looking at Logan in particular. "I've never been involved in any kind of business so it's hard for me to understand, but I know when my husband is tired out and he is so tired right now."

"Then it's good that you are feeling better," Logan observes softly. "Is Lorna still staying with you?" With Robert so busy, Logan is worried that Adrianne might be left too much on her own.

"No, she went home yesterday and started back at work today," she tells them and finally takes a seat. With her knees crossed and her leg kicking restlessly, Catherine can see that she is practically bouncing in her seat and, scarily, reminds her of the mad fairy who designed all of their wedding and bridesmaids gowns.

"You need to get out," Catherine finally tells her, and gets to her feet. "Come on, Logan can drive us all to the park and we'll take a brisk walk."

"Gladly," Logan agrees affably, having also noticed Adrianne's excessive energy. "I might even treat us all to ice-cream as this weather doesn't seem to be cooling any."

"Oh wow," Adrianne has risen and is now literally bouncing on her toes. "I'll just let Hazel know where we're going and get my bag and I must remember my mobile – I keep forgetting to take it with me," she rambles on happily. "And that's just when Robert calls, of course, so then he gets worried and I really should be more thoughtful – he has a lot on his mind lately!"

Catherine looks at Logan with wide eyes and lets out an enormous breath. "What the hell was that?! She's even worse than the mad fairy, if I didn't know better I'd think she was high!"

Laughing and putting a comforting arm about her shoulders, Logan says, "It's all perfectly normal. It's like the tears phase, pregnant women get energy spurts, days when they feel like re-organising the whole house or even redecorating it. It's just another phase."

Eyeing him sceptically, Catherine frowns up at Logan. "You seem to be very calm about this pregnancy lark, now that I think about it. You haven't fussed and fawned over me like Robert tends to with Adrianne. In fact...now that I really think about it, why not?" she asks, her frown deepening. *Ha! Answer me that, why don't you!*

His smile gives his handsome face an adoring look as the arm about her shoulder pulls her into his side. "I looked it all up on the computer – the anxiety phase, the tearfulness, the spurts of energy, the nesting behaviour and the fear of inadequacy before the birth," he tells her knowledgeably, then laughs at her look of astonishment. "What? We men have to fend for ourselves – you women go to classes and talk to each other about every little thing. If we want to know anything it's the internet or baby books."

"Baby books...?" Catherine laughs at the thought. "Did you actually buy and read a baby book?"

Logan doesn't get time to answer as Adrianne comes bouncing into the hallway. "Ready? Hazel said she'll let Robert know where I've gone if he calls the house, and dinner won't be till this evening and I'll be back by then, and then we're going to the antenatal class together. Isn't he wonderful...and after a long day at work, too!"

They watch as Adrianne bounds by them and Catherine turns to look up at Logan. "If I ever start 'bouncing' or 'boinging' around the place, you have my permission to tie me down and not let me out in public. Sheesh!"

The park is full of people enjoying the hot summer weather. Kids are playing ball, or squealing while playing chase. It all seems like such a miracle to Catherine; happy families all enjoying time together...it still feels strange to be one of them.

When a ball lands at their feet, Logan makes to kick it back but is beaten to the punch, or the kick, by Adrianne who giggles like a schoolgirl when she manages to do it right.

"Yeah!" she yells as the ball is promptly kicked back to her by the small boy who seems to think he's found a new playmate. "Here you go," and Adrianne giggles as the boy promptly returns it to her again.

"This is a whole other side of Adrianne," Catherine frowns over at her enthusiastic sister. "Is that really good for her, all that racing around?"

She tips her head up to her all-knowing husband to see him smiling contentedly watching the ball play. "She'll be fine. Adrianne's just letting off steam; she's been cooped up for weeks. But we'll go for a drink and that ice-cream I promised you in a minute or two."

In truth, he was enjoying watching Adrianne's interaction with the young boy, who he guessed was around five years old.

Will our son's love playing ball like that? Will Catherine enjoy playing with them the way Adrianne seems to? I just know she's going to be an amazing mother – even if she doesn't believe it yet.

"You look goofy happy," Catherine laughs at Logan's indulgent expression. "You're imagining our kids – which is fine," she tells him with a warning look, "as long as you see yourself chasing them around with a football at your feet. I will be teaching them to be smart," she declares, then smiles when the boy laughs at Adrianne's pathetic shot at goal. But if I do play football with them, I won't play like a girl the way Adrianne is!

When they are seated in the pavilion, their teas and coffee in front of them, Catherine begins to dwell on her conversation with Fiona that morning and Logan notices the faraway look in her eyes.

"Want to talk about it?" he asks when Adrianne goes to the ladies room.

"I don't want to spoil a lovely day," Catherine smiles dully.

"It won't spoil the day to talk to me about something that is obviously troubling you," and Logan reaches out to take her hand and give it a supportive squeeze. "It's something to do with what you're working on – have you had some bad news?"

"You could say that," Catherine frowns down into her tea, "but I'm sure Fiona Richerson would call it something much more...well..."

Taking a moment to collect her thoughts, Catherine can only imagine and sympathise with what Fiona must be going through as they sit drinking tea and coffee.

"It's Colin Richerson, Fiona's husband," she explains. "He was rushed to hospital in the night and is in intensive care. They say he had a heart-attack; probably brought on by the stress of their daughter's abduction."

"Jesus!" Logan slumps back in his chair, a hand pushing back through his wind-blown hair. "How is Fiona holding up – is there anything we can do for her?" *Besides bringing her daughter home unharmed! Shit! What a bloody mess!*

"I offered..." Catherine lifts her hands and lets them fall into her lap in a helpless gesture, "...but then, you know what I'm like with people, I probably said it all wrong and upset the poor woman even more than she was already!"

"That's complete rubbish," Logan gives her hand an annoyed shake. "The people who know you, the only ones that matter, already understand your brand of caring, and it suits them well enough!"

Giving a huffing sigh, Catherine gives Logan's shin a non-too-gentle kick to stifle the conversation at Adrianne's return.

"You ok?" Adrianne asks Logan as he frowns and rubs his sore leg.

"Mmm, just a pesky shin pain," he tells her, glancing a telling look at Catherine in the process.

"Come on, I've had enough sitting around," Catherine suddenly announces. "Let's take a walk by the lake then head back – I need to get my head into work again this afternoon."

'Breaking News!' the radio proclaims next to Mrs Baines in the kitchen of Catherine and Logan's home. 'Police have just announced that a young couple, missing for twelve days have been found. Their names have not yet been announced as the police want to inform next of kin first. Although they are alive and managed to walk free under their own steam, this reporter understands that both the male and female have been taken to hospital with various injuries and the side effects of prolonged mental and possibly even physical abuse.'

"Good Lord!" Mrs Baines declares to the empty room. "I wonder if Catherine has heard this – maybe it's that lovely young couple she's looking for!"

After arriving home, Catherine is filled in by Mrs Baines about the radio report and the young couple that have been found.

"Ok, I've just spoken to Fiona and she hasn't heard anything yet," Catherine tells Mrs Baines and Logan on returning to the kitchen. "She's been at the hospital with her husband all morning, but she's going to give the police a ring to find out what's going on."

Then Catherine turns to leave the kitchen and Logan has an idea why.

"But you don't intend to wait for her to call you back, do you?"

A gleam creeps into her eyes as Catherine turns back to look at her husband. "You know me too well. Come on, let's find out what the police know and maybe it'll help us find this bastard and put him behind bars where he belongs!"

"Don't forget me," Mrs Baines calls out. "I'll be on tenterhooks until you let me know if it's them or not."

"Will do," she hears Catherine call back as she and Logan head up to the home office. Then Mrs Baines turns back to preparing the evening meal, but has to wipe away a sudden rush of tears to see what she's doing.

Being careful not to rush the process, Catherine hacks into the police computer system and soon finds what she is looking for.

Looking up at Logan, she too has to wipe her eyes when she tells him, "It's them, Logan, it's really them."

Moving to her, Logan pulls Catherine to her feet and hugs her tight against him and feels her sobs of relief.

"These damn baby tears are driving me crazy," she excuses her uncharacteristic lack of control.

Laying his cheek on top of her head, Logan just sways with her, agrees and tells her that it will all be over soon.

"I need to ring Caroline and Adrianne too," she gulps a moment later. "They've been so worried about Natalie and Joshua, you'd think they were related."

While Catherine moves to her desk and makes a round of phone calls to let everyone know the news, Logan moves to his own desk and fires up his computer.

It's all over the news sites. No one daring to leak the names yet, but it's obvious they're talking about Natalie and Joshua.

He reads the various articles with interest, yet a nagging at the back of his mind tells him that this isn't over.

No, I don't believe this is over at all – not for Catherine and not for Natalie and Joshua either. It won't be over until the monster is found and caged – there's no hint here to indicate that anyone was caught in connection to the disappearances.

CHAPTER ELEVEN

Later that day, Logan drives Catherine and Caroline over to the hospital near Upper Stanton where the Richerson's live and where Colin Richerson is still a patient.

They find Fiona in turmoil, desperately wanting to go to her daughter, having confirmed with the police that it is indeed her daughter and Joshua who have been found, yet also wanting to stay with her critically ill husband.

"What should I do?" she asks, wringing her hands and pacing up and down the small room where her husband lies still attached to a ventilator. "My baby needs me, but so does Colin. I just don't know what to do!"

Catherine looks scared to death of the woman's neediness, but has every sympathy for her plight. Turning pleading eyes to Logan and Caroline, Catherine volunteers to stay with Colin while they take Fiona to see Natalie.

Fiona is overcome, and thanks them all for caring enough to come and help her. Logan puts an arm about the woman's heaving shoulders and Caroline holds her other hand.

When they've all gone Catherine drags a chair up to the side of Colin's bed and sits looking at the man whose heart had broken under the strain.

"She's coming home, Mr Richerson," Catherine tells the unmoving figure lying in the bed. "Your daughter is coming home. I bet she'll be in to see you as soon as she can," she says and moves to speak close to his ear. "Natalie is ok, Colin. She's safe and sound and so is Joshua. You can come back now; it's safe to wake up now."

The ventilator hisses and wheezes with every breath Colin Richerson takes, slowly, rhythmically, eerily regular.

When the monitor suddenly alarms Catherine almost jumps out of her skin and watches a nurse walk in as calm as you like.

"What the hell was that?!" she demands, backing up against a wall as far from the bed as she can get.

"Not to worry," the nurse tells her, silencing the alarm and moving wires and lines into their correct positions. "If we're not worrying then you shouldn't worry – these monitors go off just to warn us to look at something that might need tending to," the nurse explains calmly.

"So...so...he's not having another heart-attack?" Catherine gasps, her hands clutched over her own fast beating heart.

"Not at all, now don't you worry, Mr Richerson is doing fine," the nurse smiles, then restores calm and order to the room. "Would you like me to get you a hot drink – we have tea, coffee or hot chocolate if you'd like some?"

"You do?" Catherine brightens immediately. "I love hot chocolate – Logan rations me at home, says I like it too sweet and it might not be good for me or the babies. But what's the point of having chocolate if it isn't sweet, right?" Catherine demands wide eyed.

The nurse gives a chuckle and promises to return in just a minute. Then Catherine is on her own again and eyeing the now silent monitor warily.

"Just don't you go doing anything that will set those alarms off again," Catherine tells Colin, who is completely oblivious to everything going on around him, and retakes her seat at the side of his bed. "I've always hated these places," and Catherine grimaces at all the IV lines going into the side of his neck and a couple attached to needles that go right under the skin in his arms. "You've got to be a loony-toon to actually work in one of these places voluntarily – but then I suppose we'd be in a bit of a mess if everyone felt like me, hey?"

The door creaks open behind her and Catherine manages to smile when the nurse passes her a plastic cup of hot chocolate. It doesn't smell as good as the kind she keeps at home, but it's a welcome distraction from all the machines around her.

Taking a sip, Catherine is pleasantly surprised and thanks the nurse with a huge smile.

"Don't tell my husband about this will you?" she asks, taking another satisfying sip of the hot drink. Then, when the nurse shakes her head, Catherine slides down in her seat and makes herself a little more comfortable, relishing the hot sweet drink in her hands.

That evening, Catherine's lounge is full and the conversation is flowing along with the tea, coffee and wine.

Frank Harper and Sloane Shivers have joined Emma, Caroline, Catherine and Logan to discuss the progress of the investigation into the abduction murders.

"They are so traumatised by their experience, it's difficult for them to be coherent or even to remember everything," Caroline tells the group. "They won't be separated; they are in a room with two beds right next to each other and barely take their eyes off each other, even when trying to explain what happened to them."

Logan agrees, "I noticed that too. It's as though they're afraid that they'll look back and the other one will be gone."

Mrs Baines has just put a tray of hot drinks down on the central coffee table when she overhears Logan's comment.

"If you'll excuse me commenting," she begins cautiously, "but that's exactly what they are likely to be feeling. They were disappeared in the middle of the day; one moment they were having fun, had a family they would be going home to when the day was done – the next, they were nothing and no one, just an object of amusement for their abductor. They lived with the fear of losing each other every minute of every day. It's no wonder they won't leave each other's side now."

"Of course!" Logan bats a hand to his forehead in frustration then smiles at his housekeeper. "You're a trained psychologist; you'd be an invaluable resource if you wouldn't mind helping us?"

Blushing a little, Mrs Baines moves to the side of the room and feels all eyes on her.

"Well, I could perhaps talk to the youngsters," she suggests, "help them to recall details that might be difficult for them just now. Perhaps enough to help you in finding the place where they were held – is that the sort of thing you mean?"

"I do," Logan confirms. "But I also think you might be able to help us to get into the mind of the monster – he's lost a valuable prize, is under threat of discovery. What will he do? Where will he go? And will he come after Natalie and Joshua again?"

"I'd say that last point is a foregone conclusion," Mrs Baines confirms with deep concern. "He'll be angry now, probably losing his organisational skills, the skills he's needed to keep his secret hidden, to keep his captives alive for as long as he has."

Looking around the room her eyes turn sad. "If he still has any prisoners they don't have long to live. It's likely he'll take his anger out on them, in whatever way he sees fit. But I doubt their deaths will be quick from what I've seen of the torture he's inflicted on his previous victims," she observes quietly.

The silence is so loud it becomes oppressive.

"You're right," Catherine states unequivocally. "If everyone agrees, this goes 24/7 from now on." Hearing Logan's intake of breath, Catherine turns to him. "I'm not stupid – I'll rest and eat, but I'll work as hard as anyone else to get this monster behind bars and hopefully bring some of those other victims home!"

Caroline, too, is worried about Catherine's proclamation. "Look, I know nothing about computers but I can help Mrs Baines to keep you all fed and watered," she offers. "And we can take turns at getting our heads down for a while – I'll make sure Catherine sleeps when I do," she assures Logan, and sees his face relax a little.

"Good enough," he declares, and gives his wife a supportive smile. "I think we need to call in the troops," he suggests, then laughs at Catherine's stunned expression. "You know who I mean – get on the phone to lover-boy and draught him in, and anyone else you think might be able to help."

Emma's eyes fly wide as she realises what Logan has just said and who he was referring to.

Caroline laughs at her expression and simply says, "Don't ask."

Even Harper and Shivers agree to take shifts in the combined effort that is being put together.

The large house becomes a base of operations. As well as pulling Ben and David into the fray, Catherine also commandeers all of the works computers and asks them to bring their personal computers with them as well.

The large library is set aside as a coordination room — tables are brought in and laptops are set up. All the information from the upstairs office is brought down and stuck on the larger wall.

Catherine lets Frank and Sloane organise the information, as it's something they are more skilled at doing. This is, after-all, a police investigation first and foremost — but if they'll accept outside help then Catherine is more than happy to furnish it.

By midnight, Catherine and Caroline are taking their first turn in the bedrooms. Back to back, they sleep on Catherine and Logan's large double bed. In the room next to them Emma is also taking a couple of hours down.

In the library the men are still hard at it. Mrs Baines brings in another tray of refreshments, and when she's set it down walks over to look at the information wall.

"Some of these poor souls have been missing for two months," she states, her head shaking in wonder. "I don't know whether to wish them dead already or to still be alive and waiting to be found."

"I know what you mean," Detective Shivers sips on a fresh mug of tea. "But with counselling, hopefully, we can restore those still alive back to their families — we just have to find them first."

Ben is pounding away on his laptop, his fingers dancing furiously across the keys.

"I think I might have found something here," he announces after another flurry of finger tapping.

Frank and Sloane move to stand either side of him and Logan stands at his back. "What is that?" Sloane asks when he sees a field with old aircraft hangers, and a building that is all but falling down, on Ben's computer screen.

"It's an old airfield – last used officially in the Second World War. But look at this," Ben points to a chapter describing the airfield and its role in the war. "It has an underground bunker – it doesn't go into size or location, but it's a good bet you would access it from inside that building."

Frank and Sloane look at each other and nod. The airfield is a good 20 miles from where the young couple were picked up, but then Natalie and Joshua said they felt like they had been walking for miles and had even snuck onto the back of an open-backed builder's truck to get away.

That could have taken them miles away from where they had escaped, and the police were still trying to track the vehicle down to see where they might have climbed into it. But they'd had no luck so far.

"I think we should call this in," Sloane suggests. "We can get the local police to check it out and get back to us."

"What! We don't get to go?" Ben asks, disappointment etched on his tired face.

It's Frank Harper who puts the lid on that idea. "No. Absolutely not!" he proclaims firmly. "We shouldn't be involving civilians in this enquiry, let alone taking them into a dangerous situation that could put their lives in serious jeopardy!"

"I suppose," Ben reluctantly agrees.

Sloane has already moved over to the window and is deep in conversation with someone at the station. "Don't ask..." they hear him tell someone, "...just get onto the local police and get the place searched. Get back to me as soon as you know anything!"

The two police officers exchange troubled looks. "It's going to be sticky explaining where we got that tip from," Sloane tells his boss. "They were already asking some awkward questions, but I think the 'anonymous tip' should cover it."

"If we come up trumps no one will care where the information came from," Frank Harper declares.

Time drags. At four in the morning Catherine, Caroline and Emma get up to start their shift in the library.

"Why didn't you wake me?" Catherine demands when news of the airfield search reaches her ears.

"There was no point," Logan replies logically, quietly. "We don't even know if they found anything yet!"

Ben has refused to take his turn to sleep; he wants to be around when the result of the airfield search comes in. But David and Inspector Harper both go up for a power nap, with Sloane following shortly after, making sure his mobile is on the pillow next to him.

It is morning before a report gets back to Sloane. Someone from the station finally calls him to let him know that the airfield is now a crime-scene.

The monster wasn't found at the site, but it was obvious that he had operated from there at some time in the recent past. Six bodies had been discovered in varying states of decomposition.

That was six more people that they could tick off their list of missing people, but it was also six more to add to the growing list of the dead.

Moving into the conservatory, Catherine and Logan take a few minutes for themselves. It feels wrong, but necessary.

"It's depressing," Catherine leans into Logan's solid strength, drawing her legs up beneath her on the cosy seating. "I was hoping to bring them home — even battered and bruised, we could have helped them get over the worst of it."

Wrapping her into his warmth and strength, Logan can only agree. "We have to try to look at the positives. With this find, the police will have more clues to follow and will close in on the monster step by methodical step."

"God, I hope so," Catherine sighs heavily and rubs a hand over her belly. "This monster was someone's son, but he grew up to hate and torture the vulnerable around him. How do we know..." Catherine turns her face up to look at Logan, "...if the child we love and raise is going to grow up to be a monster?"

"Stop it, Catherine!" Logan pulls her around to face him. "If you keep projecting onto our boys it will drive you, and me, crazy."

"But..."

"No! These monsters are usually made, not born," Logan asserts firmly. "They often evolve out of some kind of childhood nightmare that has warped their minds, or an experience that has tipped them over the edge of sanity. I won't have you thinking about our boys in the same light as this lunatic!"

Realising that she has upset him, Catherine wraps her arms around his neck and pulls Logan closer.

"I grew out of a childhood nightmare," she reminds him, "and I think I'm afraid that that will make me a bad parent." Stroking his hair, Catherine tries to pull her frantic thoughts into some order. "I want to be the best mother that our boys could ever have – but I know little about love and I've only ever seen the worst side of human nature."

Holding her away from him, Logan shakes his head. "No. No, that isn't true," he tells her. "You had a mother who loved you enough to work extra hours to give you the books you needed. You loved her, Catherine – I hear that in every tale you tell about her."

"I only ever seem to remember one tale," she frowns and sighs. "It seems to block out everything else, yet there must have been more. There must have been happier times."

"The memories are there, Catherine, you just have to take a little quiet time to think about them," Logan encourages gently.

"I remember Caroline sometimes," and her brow pulls into a frown as she contemplates the flashbacks she's been experiencing. "When Caroline first came here and stayed at the house with us, I got upset and lay on the bed upstairs and she came up and started tickling my hair – it was like déjà-vu, and the next thing I knew I was remembering when we were girls. It was weird, but lovely at the same time."

"Has it happened since?"

Catherine nods, "Quite a few times – just snatches, pictures or sounds that are suddenly so real..."

"And your father...do you have memories of him too?"

This time Catherine shakes her head, "If I have any they're buried deep. I don't even catch a glimpse of him."

"When this is all over, we'll go to Lakelands for a visit with my father and take some time to relax together," he tells her and kisses her tenderly on the forehead.

"That may not be any time soon," she smiles ruefully. "But I'll look forward to it anyway."

"Good." Logan stands and pulls Catherine to her feet. With his arms around her he just holds her to him for a quiet moment.

The morning sun peeps through the conservatory windows, casting out the shadows and filling the gloom with rays of hopeful light.

"We'd better get back," Logan eventually suggests.

"I love you, Logan," Catherine tells him, her hands reaching up to cup his cheeks. "You help me to see the brighter side of life, something I all too often forget to do."

The newsflashes from the airfield that Sloane relays to them are gruesome in the extreme. Everyone is up now and Mrs Baines is back cooking in the kitchen making a batch of eggs and bacon for everyone to eat.

Putting terrines of scrambled eggs and tomatoes on the extended dining table, with plates of bacon and racks filled with fresh buttered toast, Mrs Baines checks to see if there is anything she's missed.

Deciding the food is adequate; she goes through to the library and calls time on the frantic activities.

"Ok, time for a break!" she calls out and gains immediate quiet. "There's breakfast in the conservatory and I don't want to hear one word about the investigation while you eat it – is that clear?"

Even Logan nods his head, taken aback by his usually quiet housekeeper. But he can see the sense in her order.

They're all tired, depressed and in need of a break, however brief.

When he hears some grumbles of dissention, Logan merely walks around the room encouraging people on their way. Even swivelling chairs away from computers so that their occupants can't continue working on them.

Once in the conservatory, however, the small crowd seems to inhale the delicious aroma of bacon and eggs as one, and heave a sigh of longing in one long synchronous moan.

The conversation is lively, but not one word about the case is uttered.

"You do know we have an appointment at the hospital later today?" Caroline reminds Catherine and Logan. "We're getting photos of the babies, remember!"

Catherine scoffs loudly, "Photos of scotch mist, more like. How the hell they can tell the sex of the babies is beyond me – I can't tell their heads from their backsides, let alone what tackle they have or don't have!"

The table erupts with laughter, probably more than her comment deserved, but it was such a relief to find some humour to enjoy.

"My wife said the same thing," Frank Harper tells them all. "Of course, we didn't get photos in our day and the equipment wasn't so advanced, but the operative seemed sure they knew which bits were which and that they all appeared to be there."

"Yeah, but did you see it?" Catherine asks. "When they said, ahh look, there's his hand – did you actually see the damned hand...'cause I sure as hell couldn't make it out!"

"Well...no...," Frank has to admit, "...it was all a bit hazy."

"Scotch mist! Just like I said," Catherine affirms. "I'm not even convinced they know for sure that we're having boys!"

Logan frowns at that suggestion and pauses with a loaded fork on its way to his mouth. "Really? They sounded pretty certain. Still, it's a shame we couldn't get photos at the time – but we'll get some this afternoon, I'm sure."

Catherine just raises a cynical brow.

"So what will you do if you get one of each," Sloane asks with interest. "I mean, do you have any girl clothes just in case, or girl's names as a backup?"

Catherine looks alarmed and straight at Logan, "We only just got the boys names straight – what the heck do we do if we have a girl? We didn't buy anything for a girl," she states, panic starting to rise in her voice.

"Stop fretting," a much calmer Caroline tells her sister. "We've got loads of girl clothes and you've got loads of boy clothes – if they come out different to what we expect then we'll just have to share the clothes around for a bit."

Looking at her twin and wishing she could take the whole pregnancy and motherhood thing as calmly as Caroline, Catherine takes a deep breath and blows it out slowly.

"You're right! Of course, you're right," she tells Caroline then looks at Sloane accusingly. "What makes you such an expert? When did you have to come up with a backup name for a baby – I thought you said you were single?"

Emma's head barely lifts but Catherine sees the movement and knows she is listening to his answer with interest.

"You don't need to be married to have kids," Sloane replies candidly, and Emma sucks in a shocked breath.

"So you've got kids?" Catherine persists, frowning when he just laughs.

"I've got a niece and a nephew," he finally confesses, giving Emma a sidelong look. "I just remember my sister saying that they needed a backup name in case the Sonographer got the sex of the baby wrong."

When his mobile phone sounds, Sloane takes it out of his pocket and walks back to the library to take the call.

In the conservatory the conversation has fallen eerily quiet and everyone has stopped eating.

When Sloane walks back into the conservatory they can all see that the news is bad.

"That was a call from the airfield," he tells them, a hand sliding back through his already tousled brown hair.

"They just found another two bodies, a young couple not much older than Natalie and Joshua."

"The Taylors," Catherine suggests. "They were in their early twenties."

"Or the Phillips'," Emma recalls. "They're about the same age – 23 and 24 I think."

"There's no ID as yet," Sloane tells them all. "I'm going to get back to it, though I'll take a mug of that coffee with me if there's some going spare?"

Emma reaches over to the thermos jug and pours him a mug then walks around the table to hand it to Sloane herself.

"I'll join you," she tells him and follows him out.

CHAPTER TWELVE

"How do you know that isn't the cord thingy?" Catherine asks the Sonographer when she states with certainty that they are indeed having twin boys.

Patiently, the woman takes Catherine through each baby's anatomy, clearly pointing out what is what and where.

Catherine's eyes fly wide open, "Logan...look at that...it's our son's face...you can see it...I can see it! Oh my God!"

His eyes have teared up, but Logan can clearly see the face of his son looking right back at him from the screen.

Taking her hand, Logan gives it a squeeze and then moves in for a kiss.

"I adore you, woman, and our babies will have a wonderful mother!"

"You're sure?" Catherine looks up at her husband with all her fears laid bare in her lovely blue eyes. "You really think I can do this right?"

"I do. I absolutely do," he laughs, the joy of the moment pushing all thoughts of the work they would be getting back to right out of his heart and mind.

"Do you think Caroline is seeing her girls just like this?" she muses, not able to take her eyes off her boys.

There are two Sonographers working today, and Caroline went in to her appointment at the same time Catherine did.

"You know, I could do you a short video of the boys as well as the photographs you asked for," the Sonographer offers. "There's an additional charge for the DVD but it would be a wonderful keepsake."

Her jaw drops open, "You can do that?"

"Of course," the Sonographer chuckles, and loads a DVD into the slot and begins to record the session.

Back in the reception area, the twins meet up and both look full to bursting with happiness.

"Did you get pictures?" Caroline asks, waving an envelope containing her own baby photos about.

"We got a DVD too – I didn't even know they could do that!" Catherine laughs and gives her twin an awkward but fierce hug. "Let's go back to your place, we can look at the photos and watch the DVD's over some of that fancy tea you have."

Logan is pleased that Catherine has elected to take some time for herself. The continuing investigation into the missing couples is difficult and emotionally draining. It will do her good to get away from it, even for a short while.

Travis looks as dopey happy as Logan, both proud fathers and obviously overcome by seeing their children alive and well on the ultrasound screen.

"I can't get over the fact that I've just seen our daughters," Travis tells Logan as they walk back to the car park, their excited wives walking arm in arm leading the way. "It was incredible, even though we saw them a month ago. One of them was even sucking her thumb – can you believe that?"

Logan's eyebrows rise in surprise, "You actually saw that?"

"Plain as day," Travis tells him proudly.

"I couldn't believe the way my son looked at me, like he knew I was standing right there," Logan smiles, remembering his son's eyes open and curious. "I mean, I know he couldn't really see me, but it was uncanny when I saw his little face on the screen. His brother had his head turned, but we saw enough to know that we are definitely having twin boys," Logan laughs.

Travis actually colours up, "Yes, we got confirmation that we are definitely having twin girls, too."

For a couple of hours everyone's thoughts are on the new lives growing in the girls' wombs - new life, new hope, and a world of joy just waiting to emerge.

Photos are pawed over, oohs and aahs exchanged with regularity, but the time finally comes when it all has to be put aside.

"We need to get back," Catherine finally says what Logan knew she must. "It's been great spending time with you two, but we must get back to the investigation."

"I know Logan won't let you overwork," Travis tells Catherine as he gives her a goodbye hug, "but I'm going to say it anyway – take care of yourself and those boys, they need you too."

It was almost word for word what Logan had said when she had decided on helping Fiona Richerson find her missing daughter, and Catherine appreciated the love that was wound in between the words.

"I'll be good," Catherine tells him, and returns his hug with real enthusiasm. She's gradually getting used to being cared for by others, to having a family that truly loves her.

Back at the house, they walk into the library and find Ben with his head down on his desk and Emma still pounding away at her laptop.

"Any news?" Logan asks.

Looking tired and a little downhearted, Emma fills them in. "Frank and Sloane had to go into the station then over to the airfield – from what they've been able to tell us I'm glad going there isn't part of our remit. It sounds gruesome and soul-destroying, but I suppose they're used to it in their line of work."

"I can't imagine anyone ever gets used to it," Catherine sighs, then pokes Ben on his shoulder to wake him up. "Go to bed," she tells him when Ben looks up to see whose disturbing him. "Get some proper rest or you'll be no good to us."

"Hey, I found the airfield didn't I," he protests grumpily.

Catherine has to smile, he looks like a put-out little boy, "You did good, ace – now get some sleep and come back at it well rested. I'll be on shift now."

"Ok. Ok," Ben finally agrees, and stands up yawning and stretching out a few kinks. "I'll set my alarm for a couple of hours then I'll be back down."

"Make it three, you look like you need it," Logan advises, and smiles at Ben's disgruntled frown.

"He still has a soft spot for you," Logan puts an arm around Catherine. "And he doesn't like taking orders from me. I'll try to keep out of his way, just to keep the peace."

"This is your home," Catherine looks up at her husband and feels her heart swell with love. "Our home – if he wants to help out then he needs to respect that."

"Ok," Logan placates and places a warm kiss on her upturned lips, "but I'll just give him a bit of wiggle room so that he doesn't feel resentful. After all, I got the girl," he grins possessively, "so I can afford to be magnanimous."

"Well, your girl needs to get working," Catherine tells him firmly.

Getting back into the work, Catherine has to steel herself against the images and details that she reads in the police reports. She's looking for any detail, a connection, or mention of something that might lead them to where the current victims are being held.

Emma's right, this work can be soul-destroying – it certainly isn't for the fainthearted, that's for sure.

Nothing, she can't find anything that the police aren't already looking into.

Ok. Let's have a look at any buildings like the airfield. That underground bunker was used for war planning and safety – maybe there are more like it in the area or in the surrounding area?

After a couple of hours, she hasn't found anything new. *Right, risky or not I'm going into the government files. They have to have records of old war bunkers, communications rooms and shelters.*

Now then, let's see what we have here...

For the next hour or so she sifts through an amazing amount of information. Like the airfield, some buildings are still standing, others have been pulled down and rebuilt on, yet others have been converted for modern day use.

She's interested in the ones in out-of-the-way places, where human traffic would be negligible if not zero.

"I've found another one," she eventually tells the room. Looking up, Catherine sees Emma, Logan, Mrs Baines and Sloane Shivers looking back at her.

"What have you found?" Sloane asks, and walks over to take a look at her screen.

"I didn't realise you were back," Catherine tells him, moving back from her computer to give him a better look. "I know this site is fifteen miles from the airfield but he has transport — he must have for when he abducts his victims," she reasons.

Nodding, Sloane looks at the details on her screen then notices the files she's into. "Holy fucking Jesus! Are you trying to get yourself arrested?"

Marching across the room, Logan stands tall and broad between Sloane and his wife. "She's trying to find a murdering bastard who still has victims he's torturing on a daily basis according to Natalie and Joshua, so back off!"

Even Catherine is surprised by Logan's fierce tone and protective stance which is leaving Sloane in no doubt that he'll cause him physical injury if he even tries to arrest her.

Not quite as tall or as broad as Logan, Sloane still squares up to him. "If your wife compromises this investigation by gaining evidence illegally - evidence that we may not be able to use in court because it was gained illegally - then you can bet your arse I will arrest her."

"Sloane," Emma calls out to draw his attention, "let's just look at what Catherine has found and go from there. The victims might still be alive, but we don't know for how much longer. He's going to be pissed that Natalie and Joshua got away and he's going to be scared that they might have told us where he was holding them. He doesn't know that they couldn't and might be disposing of the evidence while we stand here arguing about it!"

Giving a snarling glance up to the giant of a man standing in his way, Sloane nods. "Ok, we look and we see, but no more hacking into government computers...understand!"

Returning his glare, Logan steps aside but only a couple of inches and doesn't relax or take his eyes off Sloane.

Reading all the info and assessing the possibilities, Sloane nods and looks at Catherine. "I'm inclined to think you may be right," he admits, then stands looking down at her. "If you're caught looking into those files, it won't be me that comes to arrest you and you won't get advanced warning either. Get yourself out and stay out," he warns. Turning, with his mobile in hand, Sloane calls in another anonymous tip.

The room remains silent then Mrs Baines crosses to Catherine. "He's a police officer through and through and seeing you flout the law, as he would see it, flies against everything he believes in." Looking up at Logan, she gives him a disapproving stare. "And, while understandable, your attitude just got his back up. Men!"

Mrs Baines goes back to her kitchen - her little domain where she rules in peace.

"That told you," Catherine laughs, getting up and slapping Logan's shoulder.

"If you could restrain yourself from hacking into government computers I wouldn't need to be told," Logan growls, still not happy at the prospect of his wife being arrested.

"I've told you before, I'm meticulously careful — no one will even know I looked," Catherine assures him, and takes a turn about the large room to stretch her back out.

A few minutes later, Sloane returns. "They're on their way. I'm picking Frank up at the airfield and then we'll be on our way too." He stops, looks at Catherine and gives a half smile. "If this pans out I'll thank you, if not...well, let's just say I'll be keeping a closer eye on you."

He turns and leaves an ominous void in his wake.

When Ben gets up, he's a little miffed to have missed all the action and possibly a little miffed that he didn't find the second location.

He'd enjoyed being the hero of the hour, but he supposes the only thing that matters is getting the missing people home safe.

That is a big ask, but every one of them is praying for it to be true.

"You've done your bit, now go and have a lie down," Logan tells Catherine when he sees her unable to stifle a huge yawn.

Her dreams are terrible. Darkness! Tunnels! Screaming!

She's running, pushing through overgrown bushes bleeding from the thorns that tear at her skin.

But the fear that is pumping adrenaline throughout her body is building, building, building, and the dark shadow is coming, closing in, reaching for her...

Logan hears her screams from the library and tears up the stairs like a man half his size. When he enters the bedroom Catherine sits bolt upright, her eyes unseeing and her terrified screams sill tearing from her throat.

Pulling her to him, Logan tries to brush away her tears but they are replaced by new ones just as quickly.

"What is it Catherine? What is it?"

"He's coming. He's coming. I feel him all around me...he's coming!"

"No, baby, no," Logan rocks her in his arms, stroking her hair and trying to still the tremors.

"He...he...he's going to kill me, he...he's going to...to rape me like he did my mother..."

"No, Catherine, Edwards is gone," Logan tells her firmly, trying to still the hysteria bubbling out of Catherine. But her head is shaking in disbelief, the nightmare still surrounding her. "He's gone, Catherine. He's gone!"

For what seems like forever, Catherine burrows into Logan and hides in his arms. His strength surrounds her, his love a warm shield that gradually eases her troubled mind and restores order to her thoughts.

"Not Edwards. Not..not Charlie Edwards," she mumbles into his saturated shirt.

"No sweetheart, he's gone now, he can't hurt you anymore," Logan's deep voice rumbles through her.

"Those people...all those poor people," Catherine moans quietly. "I could hear them screaming, then something was chasing me – I thought it was him, come back to finish me off."

"I won't let anyone hurt you, Catherine, not ever again, I swear to you."

CHAPTER THIRTEEN

Five couples – that was how many the police had found when they raided the old war-room. Some had already died from their injuries, some were close to death and yet others were almost certainly going to survive.

"There were names scratched into the walls, just like in the other place," Sloane tells them the following day. "We're going to follow up on them all, confirm who they were and if they're still listed as missing – I just can't imagine what the final head count is going to be."

"But still no sign of the monster?" Catherine asks quietly. "No concrete leads, nothing to tell us where he is now?"

Shaking his head, Sloane can only tell them what he knows for sure. "There were three people already dead at the scene – two women and a man. Another five had serious, life-threatening injuries and the other two were seriously injured but expected to survive."

Catherine stands, paces the room, then comes to a stop and looks out of the library window.

"You know where he's going," she tells Sloane Shivers, "and so do I. Have you still got Natalie and Joshua under guard?"

He'd hoped she wouldn't make the leap, but he should have known better. "Yes. They've got twenty-four hour cover – he won't get near them!"

"I hope you're right," she tells him, and turns from the window to look him straight in the eyes. "Because if he does he'll make them suffer worse than ever. He'll take his time with them; make them pay for escaping and bringing down his disgusting empire of pain and suffering."

"We've got them covered," is all Sloane can say. "I need to get back to the station, but I came here to thank you all first." Taking a step nearer to Catherine, he tells her, "What you did was stupid and illegal, but you saved lives – for that reason alone I'm going to forget what you did and trust you won't do it again. If you do, expect a knock on your door in the dead of night...it won't be me."

When everyone has gone, the house feels drained and the commotion of activity of the last couple of days feels almost dreamlike. Unreal!

At breakfast next morning, the conservatory is lit by brilliant sunshine. It should be uplifting, should be a wonderful start to a new summers day – but it feels heavy and ominous.

"I don't like to think what that monster is planning," Catherine speaks into the silence and looks over at a contemplative Logan. "He'll want revenge and be determined to get it. And he's proven already that he's nobody's fool – he hasn't gone undetected all these years by being stupid."

Logan nods and reaches over to take her hand, "You've done everything you possibly could – it's up to the police now."

"I know you're right, but it won't feel like enough if they don't get to him before he gets to Natalie and Joshua," Catherine admits sadly.

"How about doing something to take your mind off it all?" he asks with a smile that melts her insides.

"We only just got up," Catherine blushes, then blushes deeper when he laughs loudly at her.

"You've got a lovely mind, Mrs Colson-Sayers," he tells her. "But I was thinking of something to do with tackles and touchdowns, though I suppose the way we go at it sometimes the same could apply."

"You have a match?" she asks somewhat taken aback. "But, what if the investigation had still been going on?"

He knows what she is asking. "No, I wouldn't have gone off to play rugby while you were slogging away on the case," he tells her with a frown. "And I'm surprised you would even think it. I rang the captain and offered my services. I'm playing in reserve."

"Reserve! Are they crazy?!" Catherine is sat with a ramrod straight spine, indignant on his behalf.

"They can't just wait around for me to call," Logan explains reasonably.

"Reserve, ha! I'll give the girls a call and we'll get a real supporters group together. Reserve," she mutters again in disgust, and causes Logan to laugh at her umbrage.

The clubhouse is full of home and away fans having drinks and a chat before the match.

Adrianne, Robert, Caroline, Travis, Ben, David, Emma and Catherine are all sat at a table discussing the upcoming match and the fact that Logan is being played as reserve.

"I expect you all to do your bit and shout for Logan to come on," Catherine orders firmly, frowning at each of them in turn.

"If we don't get out there the match will start without us," Ben states, nodding his head in the direction of the supporters exiting the clubhouse.

"Right then! Here we go!" And Catherine leads the way with determination in every stride.

"You'd never guess she is 27 weeks pregnant with twins the way she's running up and down the line," Caroline tells the rest of the group as they watch Catherine shouting at the players, egging them on.

"If she doesn't slow down she'll do herself a damage," Adrianne frowns with concern. "Stop her, Robert – she can't be jumping up and down like that!"

Robert raises an eyebrow at his wife and then looks over at Catherine. *No one tells Catherine what to do without taking out life insurance first. But what the heck, Adrianne is right.*

Running up the sideline, Robert calls out to her, "Catherine! Hey, Catherine!" When he gets her attention Robert tries not to waver under her ferocious glare. "The girls are getting worried about you. You're poor boys are getting jostled in there," he points to her baby bulge and gives a nervous laugh.

Looking down, Catherine regards the swell of her stomach and puts a hand to it. "My boys are fine," she tells him stubbornly. "If you lot were shouting a bit louder I wouldn't have to do it all!"

Reluctantly she walks back with him to the rest of the group. Then a whoop goes up from the home supporters as Logan strides onto the pitch and Catherine again starts jumping up and down and shouting her support.

Everyone around her is alarmed, and Adrianne and Caroline roll their eyes at each other behind Catherine's back.

It doesn't take long for Logan to make his mark on the match. He's like a bulldozer the way he pushes his way forward with the ball.

Someone on the opposition takes his legs from under him and Logan falls heavily on top of the luckless player who has to be helped from the pitch.

"Serves you right," Catherine frowns at the bulldog of a man as he hobbles by her. Then she turns to smile brightly at her husband. "Go get 'em tiger!"

Giving her a wide grin, Logan jogs back into the fray and does exactly that. Catherine has to grimace at some of the scrums and tackles Logan gets involved in, and shouts at the opposition to stop playing dirty when she witnesses a boot go into Logan's ribs after a tackle that leaves him on the ground.

But she needn't have worried, in seconds Logan is up and scoring a touchdown that is its own justice. And he manages to take the man down in the next scrum with a move that leaves the home crowd cheering loudly.

Sheriton win the match 35 – 15, and Logan is cheered as a hero having scored three touchdowns and facilitated a couple of dropkicks.

The clubhouse is rocking by the time the team enter. Showered and changed, they are bought pints by their supporters and songs are sung in their honour.

On the drive home, Catherine fairly bounces in her seat with pride and enthusiasm.

"Reserve!" she scoffs. "Well you showed them!"

Laughing at her disgust and pride; Logan feels good seeing his wife all fired up and enjoying herself.

"I don't think the lads dared to let down such a ferocious supporter," he tells her, and laughs again when she turns to frown at him. "That is exactly what I mean – I think you terrified the opposition into submission with that scowl!"

"Good! But you did alright, ace," she smiles over at him. "That idiot who brought you down never came back on – knocked more than the wind out of him, didn't you!"

They both laugh and the drive home is a happy one.

When Logan pulls up on the drive, he turns to Catherine and asks, "What about a few days at Lakelands? I'm at a point where a break wouldn't cause any problems with work and you don't really have anything on that Ben and the rest can't continue to handle for a few days longer?"

Quietly, Catherine considers. The monster hasn't been caught, but there isn't really anything else she can do, is there?

What if he takes Natalie or Joshua while I'm away? I don't know that I want to be that far away – just in case.

He can see the worry chase across her face and knows what she is thinking.

"You can't put your life on hold," he tells her softly. "The truth is, they may never catch him – he's evaded them this long."

Biting down on her bottom lip, Catherine finally nods her head in agreement. "You're right, and we do need to discuss a few things with Henry."

"So we're going?" he asks, barely daring to believe that she has given in so easily.

Again, Catherine nods, "Yes, you're right, we can't put our lives on hold. I just hope Frank and Sloane do their jobs right and keep Natalie and Joshua safe."

The drive to Lakelands is light-hearted and their discussions on the way are of a future that will be centred around Logan's family home.

"I wonder what plans your dad will have come up with," Catherine speculates with a broad smile. "When I saw him going through the blueprints he seemed to have some ideas for making the house more family friendly."

"I spoke to him a couple of nights ago, about Mrs Baines living with us and the accommodation she will need," Logan explains. "He seems to have some good ideas about her living accommodations being next to an area that he thinks will make a good nursery for the boys. We'll be able to walk it through with him and make suggestions for any alterations that might need to be made."

When Lakelands comes into view their smiles outshine the sunny day.

"Home," they both say together, and laugh with shared joy.

When the front door opens, Clint, Henry's dog beats him out of it and is jumping clear off the ground in excitement as Logan's car draws up.

Wagging his tail, his whole body shaking with it, Clint bounds up to Logan and even makes him take a step back.

"Hey boy," Logan gives the dog a rough scratch behind his ears and laughs when he rolls on the ground for a belly rub.

"Hi, Henry," Catherine puts her arms around the older man's neck to give him a warm hug.

"You are coming along," Henry looks down at her baby bump with some concern. "Are you sure you still have fourteen weeks to go?"

Giving a carefree laugh, Catherine walks into the house beside her father-in-law. "Actually, it's thirteen now – I can't help counting the weeks down."

"In your position, I'd be doing the same," Henry joins in her laughter but eyes her growing stomach with some apprehension.

"Don't worry, dad, Catherine's getting the best care, and they say the pregnancy is progressing well," Logan reassures his father.

"Hmm, but won't all this upset bother you," he says, referring to the reason for their visit.

"Not at all," Catherine grins, "I'm looking forward to all the planning and making this home for the boys. It's you that should be worrying," she suggests. "After all, you've been used to a lot of peace and quiet, I can't imagine you'll be getting much of that when the building work starts and the boys arrive."

Henry gives a snort of disgust, "Peace is for the dead, and I don't plan on going anywhere until I've had a good few years with my grandsons."

"Well, as long as you're sure," Logan tells his father, following him out to the kitchen where Aida has made a fresh pot of tea. "Hi, Aida, is he giving you any trouble?" Logan asks with a nod towards his father.

"Nothing I can't handle," she smiles at Logan then pours out a mug of tea and hands it to him. "Would you like a mug?" she asks looking over at Catherine. At her nod, Aida pours her some tea and hands the mug over to Catherine. "I don't need to ask if you want a mug," Aida frowns up at Henry, "never known you to say no to a mug of tea!"

Sitting at the kitchen table the discussion starts in earnest.

"If we're going to do this we may as well do it properly," Henry states firmly. "We should have had a pool put in when you were a boy, now is the ideal time to put that right."

"A pool? What kind of a pool?" Catherine asks bemused. "Can't we just buy them a paddling pool when they get big enough?"

"What?" Henry almost chokes on his tea and Logan has to swallow down hard on a laugh knowing that Catherine would be embarrassed.

"He's talking about a swimming pool," Logan clarifies, "and I must say I agree - if we're going to get the builders

+in we may as well get it all done at once."

Catherine's eyes are goggling, her glance flicking between Logan and his father, but she decides to say nothing. This is going to be a whole new world for her to live in. She was not brought up in wealth and privilege, but realises that her sons will be.

"I was wondering about a gym," Logan suggests. "I could give up my town membership and train at home - especially if we're getting the pool done too."

"There's plenty of room for both at the back of the house - we can get full length French-doors put in to lead out to the garden."

"Just make sure the gym and pool doors have childproof locks on," Catherine tells them. "I may not know much about children but I know they get into places they shouldn't and both the gym and the pool would be dangerous places for them to wander into."

Nodding solemnly, Logan agrees. "That's a must! Don't worry, Catherine, we'll make sure it's all child friendly."

"So, what were your thoughts on the nursery idea?" Henry asks with a raised eyebrow.

"I think we'll need to walk it through - Catherine doesn't know the house that well, and even I'm having difficulty picturing the rooms you mean," Logan frowns over at his father.

Finishing their tea, the three of them walk back to the grand entrance hall and go up the main staircase.

"Ok, I was thinking that, if I move into the master suite in the west wing you could take over the master suite in the east wing which has access to what used to be the nursery when you were a boy," Henry explains, and opens the large double doors to a wonderful suite of rooms that he currently occupies.

"You'll have your own double bathroom, a private sitting room and the nursery adjoins the bedroom," Henry looks at Catherine to see what she thinks as they do a walk through.

"Henry...we can't just turf you out of your own rooms," Catherine begins, but if he is willing she knows the situation would be perfect for them.

"This is a family suite, and that's just what you'll be," he grins happily at Catherine, and she knows then that he is happy to be making the changes for them.

"You also had ideas for Mrs Baines, I think," Catherine adds after taking a good look around what will soon be her new home.

"Yes. There are some more rooms on the opposite side of the nursery," Henry tells them, and leads the way out and down the corridor to another, smaller suite of rooms. "This also has a small sitting room and an en-suite bathroom, just not on the same scale as the master," he explains as they walk from room to room.

"Does that door connect to the nursery?" Catherine points across the bedroom.

"Yes, that's right," Henry confirms. "The nursery is effectively sandwiched between this suite and your own, having access on both sides."

Looking around the rooms, walking through to the nursery then through to the master suite on the other side, Catherine finds herself to be the centre of attention with both men watching her expectantly.

"What?" she asks them nervously.

"Well...will it do?" Logan asks. "You can decorate it however you please - but will the layout work for us?"

In that moment Catherine realises that there isn't much either man wouldn't do to make her happy. This is a monumental moment in their lives and she holds the final say in making it happen.

"Well of course it will work - it's absolutely amazing," she tells them wide eyed and happy beyond belief. "With just one little proviso," she amends. "You have to let me get Caroline, and maybe Adrianne, involved with the decorating - I hate that sh...I...I mean, I'm no good at that stuff," Catherine amends quickly, causing both Henry and Logan to laugh out loud.

Blushing wildly, Catherine leads the way back downstairs.

Aida takes one look at Catherine's scowl and decides to get on with cooking the evening meal.

When the men follow into the kitchen a minute later, they are deep in conversation about the rugby match that Logan's team had won earlier in the day.

Catherine eventually moves off into one of the cosier sitting rooms and phones Caroline.

"Hey, how are you doing?" she asks her sister.

"I'm fine, you?" Caroline asks in return.

"I'm fine – I just called to ask a huge favour," Catherine admits with a grimace that her twin can hear in her voice. "We're at Lakelands and Henry just showed us a massive suite of rooms that will be ours when we move down here. There's a nursery too, and a smaller suite of rooms for Mrs Baines – trouble is they all need decorating."

"How is that trouble?" Caroline asks, then realises who she's talking too. "And that's the huge favour? You want me to help you chose some of the fittings?"

"Err, I want you to do it all — choose whatever decorating, fittings, carpets and whatever the hell else needs choosing and get whoever in that needs to do it!" *Damn it! Just the thought of getting my head into any of that stuff is enough to give me a headache!*

"You mean, I get to spend thousands of pounds of your money on whatever I please to decorate about a half-dozen rooms?" Caroline asks with a note of manic glee in her voice. "Of course I'll do it. When do I start?"

Catherine laughs with relief and pulls her feet up under her on the settee. "Jesus you're weird — if I didn't know I was speaking to my sister I'd worry that you'd been replaced by an alien!"

"Are you kidding me?! I love fashion and coordinating — doing up what will essentially be your home will be a pleasure, and in a very real sense an honour."

"Ok. Right. Well, what about coming down here tomorrow with Travis? This place has hundreds of bedrooms," Catherine exaggerates wildly. "And you could ask Adrianne and Robert if they want to come too — she's as into all that coordinating stuff as you are!" she states, unable to hide the note of disgust in her voice.

"Hmm, Travis will love the idea – he's often talked about Lakelands after staying there for Logan's bachelor night. But I don't know about Adrianne and Robert – he's still working the clock round."

"Is he leaving Adrianne on her own in that bloody great house?" Catherine asks, concern for her baby sister coming out as an angry demand.

But Caroline just tut-tuts it away. "Stop panicking – Adrianne is never alone in that mansion; it takes a small army of staff to run it and quite a few actually live in."

"All the same, they're not family," Catherine asserts hotly. "You make her see reason and bring her with you or I'll drive back up there and do it myself!" *Damn man putting his business before his pregnant wife! I'll have to get Logan to have words with him – and if he doesn't I flaming well will!*

"Stop getting your knickers in a twist," Caroline tells her firmly. "I'll ask Adrianne to come down with us, and Robert too if he can make the time," she assures her sister. "Are you sure Logan's dad won't mind us all descending on him?"

"He loves having visitors," Catherine grins happily. "I think he's missed having people around him. And anyway, you're family," she adds, as if that says it all. And in Catherine's world, it does.

CHAPTER FOURTEEN

The rest of the afternoon and evening pass in a haze of conversation about the various plans for the houses' overhaul and laughter about what trouble the boys are likely to get in to.

"You used to frighten your mother half to death when you started climbing trees and skinning your knees," Henry recalls fondly. "I don't expect your boys will be any different."

"Of course they'll climb trees," Catherine asserts with expectant pride. "And Logan will build them a tree-house too – you know, I always loved reading about those. It would be cool for the boys to have their own space."

Logan looks at Catherine with all the love in his heart shining out of his soft brown eyes. She had barely had a childhood, but she was already planning to make their boys' one to remember.

"I don't know about building one myself, but I'll certainly make sure they get one," Logan grins over at his wife.

"Good enough," Catherine grins back. "And one of those knotted swing ropes, you know – you tie it from a tree branch and it has a huge knot at the bottom that you sit on."

"Anything else?" Logan asks fondly.

"Well you were a boy once, don't you have any ideas?" she asks with raised brows.

"I'll put my mind to it and let you know," he tells her.

"By-the-way, I forgot to tell you that Caroline rang me back," Catherine says with a grin as wide as the lake the house is named after. "She said she and Travis will bring Adrianne and Robert with them and they'll get here about noon tomorrow. Is that still ok?" she asks looking at Henry.

"Couldn't be better," the older man replies. "This house was meant for family!"

"That's just what I said," and Catherine really begins to feel that she is making the right choice to move into Lakelands.

It isn't really late when Logan takes Catherine up to bed. But he's seen the way her shoulders have begun to sag and her eyes drift shut when she thinks no one has noticed.

"It isn't even eleven o'clock," she protests when they reach the bedroom.

"You three need a good night's sleep," Logan tells her and wraps her in a loving embrace as they stand looking out the window and across the beautiful moon-lit lake.

"This will be our home soon," she croons, leaning her head back against Logan's chest.

"You really seem to have taken to the idea," he says, and lays his cheek on the top of her hair.

"I have – and don't ask me why. It just feels so right."

"It does to me too." When she turns in his arms, Logan moves to kiss her upturned lips. "I love you, Catherine, and I'll do whatever I can to make you and the boys happy here."

"Right now, what would make me happy is if you stopped talking and used that gorgeous mouth on me instead!"

On a low chuckle, Logan does her bidding and kisses her so thoroughly that her knees begin to buckle.

"Wow! I am so full of good ideas today," Catherine groans against the corner of his mouth.

"I have plenty of my own," Logan states, and sweeps a hand behind her knees to lift her into his arms. "To bed with you woman and let me love you."

And he does. Thoroughly. Tenderly. Earth-shatteringly.

By noon, Catherine is like a cat-on-a-hot-tin-roof. She can't sit still and fidgets about so much that Logan eventually grabs her hand and takes her out for a walk.

"You need to walk off some of that pent up energy," he tells her, making sure she's wearing a hat as the sun is high and hot today.

"I just want them to get here already," Catherine moans, and keeps turning to look up the long driveway. "She said they'd be here by noon – it's quarter past already!"

"Not everyone is as literal as you," Logan rebukes her gently. "They probably just had an errand or two to do before they set off or on the way - nothing to get excited about, anyway."

"Not for you, maybe," she frowns up at Logan. "But for me...well...this is my family visiting my new home – I've never had a home like this before!"

She sounds cross, but Logan knows it's just her way of dealing with uncertainty. And he's touched, once again, by the knowledge that Catherine has missed out on so much that most people take for granted. When she says she hasn't had a home like this before, he knows she isn't referring to the grandeur of Lakelands – she is referring to something much more simple and basic.

Catherine has never had a family home like this before – hadn't even known she had a family until a year ago when he had found out about her father and a sister.

And wasn't that a day to remember. When he'd given her a car for her birthday present then suggested she might like to drive it that afternoon to pick her sister up from the airport, she had almost literally torn his head off his shoulders.

But it had all worked out for the best in the end, and Logan smiles to himself at the memory.

"There!" Catherine shoots out an arm, pointing to a car pulling into the gates and making its way to the house. "Come on!" And she drags on Logan's arm to make him move faster.

The three girls bump bellies and hug as best they can amid excited laughter and loud chatter.

"Did you hit traffic on the way down?" Logan asks the other two men as Travis and Robert alight the car.

"No, the girls wanted to stop on the way to get you and Catherine a housewarming present – even though you haven't moved in yet," Robert adds with an indulgent shake of his head.

"They are excited alright," Travis grins over at the three women, all glowing and all very pregnant.

"Come on in out of that heat," Henry calls from the doorway. "You'll be fainting if you stay out in it too long."

Arm in arm the sisters enter the grand oak doors and follow Henry through to the kitchen.

"Aida came in especially today and has made lunch for everyone," he tells them, and gives the gruff housekeeper a smile of thanks.

"I can serve it up in the dining room if you want," Aida tells him, then starts loading terrines onto a hostess trolley to take them through when he nods in agreement.

Ten minutes later and they are all seated at one end of a very large dining table. The chatter is happy and inane, and Henry is in his element.

The walls of Lakelands are reverberating with the sounds of happy people, of exciting ideas in the making, plans for the future, of family making this house their home.

"I hear you've been extra busy of late," Logan tells Robert and watches the younger man nod in agreement.

"I haven't stopped," Robert admits. "The business is expanding – we've opened up offices in America and the setup process has been extremely demanding."

Catherine's head shoots up at the mention of America. "You'd better not be planning to steal my sister away from me!" she warns, not a trace of a smile on her fiercely protective face.

Logan can feel a potential argument brewing and makes to head it off but Robert beats him to it.

"Not at all," he smiles, undaunted by Catherine's glare. "I've already got a head of operations in place – it's been the planning and implementing that has taken my time. You don't need to worry, Catherine, we're not going anywhere."

"Good!" That one word spoke volumes, though Catherine's frown didn't lift for some time and her eyes kept glancing back at Robert suspiciously.

"Do you think I would be spending all my time on the renovations to the house if we were going to up and leave it?" Adrianne asks. "Believe me, it's no small task, even with the help of a historical architect and traditional tradesmen who actually seem to know what they're doing."

"It wouldn't be so bad if you weren't doing it all by yourself!" Catherine states with another hot glare at Robert.

As soon as the meal ends, the girls move into the smaller sitting room and the men go off to the snooker room for a relaxing game or two.

"You two settle in, I'm just going to help Aida with the pots and I'll bring us all some tea in," Catherine suggests, and settles into the role of hostess without even realising it.

"So, Catherine's as lively as ever." Robert leans over the snooker table and prepares to make the break. "I suppose it keeps life interesting."

Logan laughs and gives a rueful shake of his head, "There is certainly nothing boring or everyday about Catherine. She's a one-off alright...and she's mine!" he states with real pride.

"I can't complain about Caroline, either," Travis tells them as he pours himself a club soda. "She isn't half the pistol that Catherine is, but believe me, she has her moments."

Nodding, Logan gives Travis a knowing smile. "Are you trying to say that life is dull with Adrianne?"

"Good God no!" Robert exclaims. "I heard her talking to one of the workmen the other day – it seems he mistakenly took her for a pushover who he could wind around his little finger. Boy did she ever prove him wrong," Robert grins with pride. "Apparently, he tried getting away with using the wrong type of plaster in one of the rooms and Adrianne noticed. She gave him a chance to put the mistake right but when she saw that he was continuing to use the cheaper substitute and tried to pass it off as the real thing, she chewed him out good and proper then turfed him off the job!"

"Sounds like she had good cause," Travis put in, and he too looks proud of Adrianne.

Henry pours himself a pint of beer and offers to do the same for the other men. Travis holds up his barely touched club soda to say that he is fine but Robert and Logan both say yes to a pint of lager.

"Sounds to me like all the sisters have a strong spine," Henry observes while putting the first pint on top of the bar. Then he takes another glass down to pour a second pint. "Nothing wrong with a strong woman – my Ellie was just the same; she knew exactly what she wanted and if she didn't get it the world had better duck and run!"

"So, what do you reckon the kids will be like?" Robert frowns over at Henry with mild fear in his eyes.

"I think they'll have the business heads of their fathers and the hearts and stubborn minds of their mothers," Henry laughs heartily.

"Well, here's to fatherhood," Logan holds up his pint and waits for the other men to do the same with their drinks. "Cheers!"

After a family breakfast in the dining room, Robert takes Adrianne for a walk around the lake, Travis and Logan have a rematch at snooker, and Henry chats with the twins in the kitchen.

"So, is there anything you wouldn't want me to do with the decorating?" Caroline asks Henry. "I know Catherine couldn't give a damn as long as it isn't bright pink with yellow polka dots," she tells him, giving her sister a knowing smile.

"Not really – Catherine says you have good taste, and if she trusts you then so do I."

"Hmm, that means I really do have a free hand," Caroline grins almost maniacally.

"Only, don't go too girly or over the top," Catherine warns. "This is Logan and the boys' home too; I want them to feel comfortable in it."

"Comfortable!" Caroline raises affronted eyebrows at her twin. "I do not do comfortable!"

Frowning, Catherine starts to feel a bit scared of Caroline's sometimes wild ideas. "You said you could do this, make it a family home for us and the boys – and you can bet Mrs Baines won't want bright pink with yellow polka dots either!"

Rolling her eyes, Caroline shakes her head in despair. "I do stylish, luxurious and sumptuous," she states each word precisely. "As for Mrs Baines, she'll think she's died and gone to luxury heaven."

Catherine looks to Henry for help but, being a man of the world and wise to boot, he declines to give his opinion.

"Anyone for another cup of tea?" he asks instead, and makes his escape to the kitchen.

The following day they all head back to Sheriton. Henry is smiling brightly as he waves them off, knowing that he will be seeing them all again very soon.

Having nodded off to sleep in the car, Catherine feels Logan gently nudging her awake.

"Ok, I'm just dozing a bit," she yawns loudly.

"Don't give me that," Logan chuckles softly, "you were snoring a minute ago."

Her eyes go wide, as she looks up at him. "I do not snore! I've never snored," she insists as she slams the car door shut and walks to their front door.

Logan laughs at her haughty insistence, her head held high and proud.

"How do you know – you're fast asleep when you do it," he laughs again, turning the key in the lock and pushing the front door open for her to walk ahead of him.

Catherine suddenly stops and Logan has to stop her from falling headlong as he careers into her.

"What the..." But Logan doesn't continue as Catherine wheels in his arms and slaps a hand over his mouth.

"Someone is here," she mouths the words.

Shaking his head in amusement, he pulls her to stand upright and rolls his eyes above the hand she is still holding over his mouth. "It's just Mrs Baines," he playfully whispers when he manages to pull her hand away from his mouth. "I asked her to come in today so that we could discuss whatever was decided by our visit to Lakelands."

Jumping away from him, her cheeks livid with embarrassment and anger, Catherine stands with her hands on her still slim hips, causing her baby bump to become even more pronounced. "You idiot. My heart is in my mouth and I just lost at least five years off my life...and you're...you're laughing at me! Damn it, Logan!"

Turning to stalk away from him, Catherine isn't quick enough. "Hold it!" Logan catches her around the waist, hauls her into his arms and kisses her until all signs of temper are gone.

She becomes soft and pliant in his arms, her own winding around his neck actually holding him to her. Then the devil in her takes over.

Laugh at me, will you? I don't think so!

Groaning into his mouth, Catherine deepens the kiss until Logan is putty in her hands, then she calmly steps out of his arms and leaves him gaping after her.

"Mrs Baines, hi," he hears her greet the housekeeper then has to give his head a shake to clear the sexual fog she's caused and drags in a much needed breath then lets it out slowly.

"You minx," he utters under his breath. Calmly, he walks out to the kitchen, greets Mrs Baines then smiles with narrowed eyes at his smug wife. "That wasn't very nice of you."

With her cheeks rapidly pinking up, Catherine moves into the conservatory and sits on one of the cosy seats to look out over the garden.

Logan follows her in, then sits opposite rather than next to her...and doesn't say a word.

Feeling guilty now, and more than a little turned on by her own actions, Catherine tries not to squirm under his persistent gaze.

"Ok! Maybe I shouldn't have...you know," she squirms anyway, "but you started it! You put the fear of the devil into me and then you laughed!"

"Very ungallant, I admit," but Logan still looks hurt and Catherine feels no less guilty.

Frowning, not sure how to set things right, Catherine suddenly grins while her eyes grow hot. "I'll make it up to you...we can have hot sweaty monkey sex as soon as Mrs B goes home."

Instead of jumping at her offer as Catherine expects, Logan slowly stretches his long legs out in front of him and appears to relax back into his seat.

She watches him open mouthed, it has never failed before. *Damn it!* Then another idea crosses her mind. "I'll even wear the red baby-doll set you get off on."

Now Catherine can see a gleam enter his eyes and a smile tug at his lovely soft lips.

"Pervert!" she smiles at him then squeals when, lithe as a panther, he leaps up and sweeps her into his arms.

"That offer is too good to wait for," he tells her, then carries her through the kitchen, smiles and jiggles his eyebrows at a laughing Mrs Baines and continues up to their bedroom.

Batting at him, and trying to twist out of his arms only causes them to tighten around her.

"Put me down, you pervert," she tells him when Logan kicks the bedroom door closed behind them.

But he just holds her then lowers his head to take her mouth and swallow her protests.

His lips move soft and warm in a dance that she can't help but go along with. Her moans are genuine now, her anger flowing out of her and turning into red hot passion instead.

When he is sure Catherine is hooked, he allows her body to slowly slide down his and helps her to stand on her own two feet.

Stand is probably not how Catherine would describe what she is doing. As the kiss continues she feels she is floating six feet off the ground.

His lips cause every part of her body to throb, and when his hands start to explore those sensitised parts she shudders and presses harder into him.

Clothes fall off them, revealing the feast below and their mouths devour greedily.

"On the bed," someone groans out. And as if by magic, that's where they find themselves.

When her lips part this time, it is to take him on a journey of need and lust and mind-blowing passion that is almost his undoing. Catherine needs to show him, needs to love him, just simply needs him...

But he wants to love her too. He hauls her up his body and onto her side, it's his turn now.

All thoughts of the red baby-doll nightie are long forgotten, only heat and need are on their minds.

His mouth ravages her, his tongue plundering and driving her wild. Her screams only urge him on, and he is hard as rock when he rears up, lifts her hips off the bed and thrusts deeply into her.

It is so often like this. They have only to touch to lose control, to need so desperately that life no longer depends on their next breath, it depends on that next touch, their mating of mouths and bodies that sates their very souls.

This is what love does to them...for them.

The explosion of their passions is powerful, heart-felt and all encompassing. This is what Logan will defend with his life – his woman, his soul-mate, his reason for living at all!

And God help anyone who tries to harm or take her from him!

CHAPTER FIFTEEN

The nightmare is not vague in the least. The monster is back and he's hungry for blood.

Catherine can feel him crawling through her veins, his evil gripping her heart and squeezing the breath from her lungs.

She can see a house, through his eyes she watches the lights go out and feels the gallop of his pulse as his excitement grows. Then she looks at the police in their unmarked patrol car, and she knows they are going to die.

She tries to warn them — *the monster is coming, the monster is coming* — but her voice doesn't come out of his mouth. She is trapped inside his head, his hand curving around a knife and she feels it in hers...

"Catherine! Catherine! Come on, wake up! Wake up, damn it!"

Logan is frantic, his wife is screaming and white as a ghost and he can't wake her.

"Wake up now...Catherine, please wake up! Listen to my voice. It's Logan, sweetheart, listen to Logan and wake up!"

"Oh, thank God!" His oath is torn from him as her screams die down and her eyelids flutter open. "Thank God! You gave me the fright of my life," he tells Catherine as he rocks her in his strong protective arms.

For long moments she lies there, unable to pull her mind back from the nightmare – but had it really been a dream.

Just a dream. Just a bad, awful dream. But what if it wasn't? It felt so real, that knife in my hand...no his hand. It was his hand and his eyes...no...that can't be! But what if it was...? What if what I saw was real?

"We need to call Frank or Sloane," Catherine pulls up and out of Logan's arms. "Don't ask me how I know, but Natalie is in trouble, they need to get over to her house pronto!"

In a daze, Logan watches his wife, a wife he had been terrified was being taken from him while she slept just moments ago, dash around the room pulling on clothes, any clothes, and all the while telling him that Natalie is in danger.

"Move it, Logan! Now!"

Before he can utter another word she has gone down stairs and he has to drag on clothes then run after her.

"What the hell is this all about?" he asks when he catches up to Catherine already on the phone in the sitting room.

"Please, don't question me about it," she tells a groggy voiced Sloane. "Just get over there, but not alone. Don't go into the house alone – he may still be in there!"

Once the receiver is back in its cradle, Logan crouches down in front of Catherine with deep furrows between his brows.

"What is it, Catherine? What is it you think is happening to Natalie?"

Reaching to hold his hand with both of hers, Catherine tries to explain, her blue eyes imploring him to believe her. "I saw him. No, no, that's not right, I was him – he is outside of Natalie's house, he has a knife and I'm pretty sure the police in the cop car outside her house are dead by now."

Still frowning, and still unnerved by the earlier experience of trying to wake Catherine from her nightmare, Logan can't quite take in what she is saying.

"You think you saw this in some dream?" he asks cautiously.

"No! Yes! Maybe!" she cries, then pushes up and has to stride around the room just to get rid of all her pent up energy. "I don't know what you'd call it – it's happened before, but nothing as vivid as this, nothing as real and frightening as this!"

Now Logan is standing and he's looking at her like he doesn't know her anymore.

"Stop looking at me like that! Like I'm some kind of freak!" she yells at him. "Well now you know – they didn't just call me a freak because my IQ was bigger than theirs," she tells him, referring to the kids at school who had taunted her for all of her childhood. "It didn't happen very often – and I mostly didn't believe in it anyway – but sometimes I said things that came true, and the kids hated me for it!"

He still hasn't said a word and she begins to panic, but pride holds her back from begging, "Do you want me to leave?" Her heart is breaking but her head goes up and her stubborn chin juts out.

Her words seem to bring him back from some daze-like state. "Leave! What the hell are you talking about?"

"Well, you haven't said anything, I thought you were thinking that I'm a freak too, and maybe you want me to leave?"

But I hope you don't. I love you more than life, more than I could have ever imagined loving anyone, ever. Don't turn me out now...please, Logan, not now!

Instead of the angry words she is dreading, Logan simply strides over to Catherine and wraps her in his arms.

"You scared the shit out of me when I couldn't wake you," he tells her, forgetting her embargo on profane language. "Now you talk about leaving...?"

Burrowing into him as much as her pregnancy will allow, Catherine holds on to Logan with all her heart.

"I will never leave you, but I thought...now that you know...maybe..." She can't finish the awful thought, it is too painful to put into words.

"You had a dream, that's all," he soothes, his cheek now lying against her silky blonde hair. "Shush now, and let it go. I've got you, baby, I've got you now."

I could let it go. I could just pretend it was a dream, that it didn't really mean anything at all – but it would be a lie. And when Sloane finds what I know he will, it will all come out anyway.

Better to do it now. Better he hear it from me and be able to make up his mind about our future before others get involved.

"It wasn't a dream, Logan. It's happened before," she tells him, and finally finds the will to push out of his protective arms to stand facing him.

Pushing a hand back through his floppy hair, Logan has to take a minute to assimilate his thoughts. "You really believe you can 'see' things?"

She nods then takes a seat on the nearby settee. "I can count on one hand the number of times it's happened to me, and I wasn't always asleep when it did." Catherine looks up to see his reaction.

"When was the last time?" he asks, having taken a seat in a nearby chair instead of next to her on the settee, she notices.

"Before my mother's murder."

Just four words, but they hang in the air like a death knell.

When he finally speaks, Logan isn't really sure what to say, "Was it about the murder, or did you see something else?"

"It was the murder," Catherine confirms his worst fear. "I was nine, and I was asleep. I remember my mother trying to wake me – I think maybe she found it difficult as you did tonight – and she was crying. But the dream didn't want to let me go, I could feel it pulling me back, my eyes were seeing two different images, flashing back to the dream and then to her face – it was the scariest moment of my life. Until it came true!"

"Jesus!" *Am I ever going to get to the bottom of this woman – her past, her fears and now her dreams! But leave...how can she even think I would want to lose her...she's part of me now.*

"There is no leaving each other, Catherine," Logan's rich brown voice declares quietly. "We are more joined than a pair of Siamese twins – our very souls are bound together – don't you feel that?"

A tear slides unheeded down her pale cheeks, "I hoped, but I daren't do more than that," she tells him honestly.

But they don't get to declare their undying love any more profoundly; the telephone is shrill and loud in its insistence to be answered.

Logan crosses the room while Catherine stays seated, frozen and barely breathing.

"Ok, I'll tell her...no, she isn't available right now," Logan looks over at Catherine and decides to run interference until she is more herself. "You can speak to her later, or she can call you if that's easier?"

When he turns to face her, Catherine can see that the dream was no dream and the reality hits.

It starts with a shudder then builds to racking shivers that have her teeth rattling in her jaws.

Moments later she is pulled onto Logan's lap and he absorbs her tremors until they still.

"Is she dead – did he get to Natalie?"

Logan's arms tighten about her, "She wasn't there, but her mother and father were."

Her sobs are hot and rack her as thoroughly as the shivers had just moments before. All he can do is hold her and offer comfort when she's ready to receive it.

After a long shower, Catherine is feeling more herself, but the bone deep sadness doesn't lift.

"I can't put it off any longer – I'm going to have to phone Frank or Sloane and give them some kind of explanation," she tells Logan in their bedroom.

"And have you thought about what you'll say?" he asks, worried for her peace of mind.

"I...no...not really," Catherine confesses, sitting down on the bed next to Logan. "Don't suppose you have any bright ideas to get me out of this mess?"

Shaking his head, Logan leans his forehead down to rest against Catherine's. "I don't think I've gotten my own head around the idea yet – but we'll come up with something," he assures her with a smile.

Raising her hand to touch his cheek, Catherine looks deep into his eyes and sees his soul. "Such a caring man; nothing seems to phase you where I'm concerned – I believe you may really and truly love me."

"I do!" he tells her fiercely, his lips taking hers and branding her soul with the kiss.

"I...I...believe you," she gasps when their lips finally part.

"Good! Then that's one positive thing to come out of this!" he states firmly. "Now we just have to deal with the knock-on effects."

"Sloane Shivers," Catherine moans quietly.

"Sloane Shivers," Logan confirms, only his voice is more determined and in control. "We'll invite him over for a little chat, and if he knows what's good for him he'll agree to put your call down to his 'anonymous informer'," Logan almost growls the words out.

By the time Frank Harper and Sloane Shivers arrive at the house, Logan and Catherine are standing shoulder to shoulder in a firm line of defence.

"You honestly want us to believe that you dreamed the whole thing up, that you weren't involved in any way?" Sloane demands hotly.

Logan's usually soft brown eyes are blazing and his 6 feet 4 inches and considerable girth of muscle are standing right in front of Sloane just daring him to make a move to arrest Catherine.

"She just told you, and so did I," Logan almost breathes fire down on the man who is calling his wife a liar. "She woke up from a nightmare and then called you – end of story!"

Frank Harper dares to take his life in his hands and moves to stand between the two men. "I have actually worked with a genuine psychic before," he tells Sloane, "so it isn't beyond the realms of possibility!"

Taking a step back, Sloane looks up at his boss with incredulity written all over his handsome face. "You actually believe in that bullshit!"

Catherine moves to remonstrate with Sloane over his language, but Logan pushes her back behind him and she takes the hint, but still holds her hands firmly over each side of her stomach to protect her babies' ears.

"Watch your language," Logan tells him instead, "there's a lady present!"

Sloane actually stops in mid tirade, and rolls his eyes. "Apologies, I'm sure. Now let's get real, Frank, you don't honestly believe all this bullsh...this rubbish," Sloane corrects himself having heard Logan's growl.

"I rather think I do, in fact," Frank Harper looks up at Logan and then around him at Catherine. "I'm not as closed minded as some, and a lot less cynical than others."

That statement seems to drain Sloane of his anger, but is quickly replaced by disbelief. "You say you've worked with a psychic – I never heard about it?" he tells his boss sceptically.

"I am not a psychic!" Catherine states loudly and pushes her way out from behind Logan. "I just have, the odd...insight," she eventually explains, though all Sloane does is raise an eyebrow at her.

"Insight! Foresight! It's the same damn thing...," Sloane rages, "...when you're talking about seeing things before or whilst they are happening!"

"The main question is, what do you intend to do about it?" Logan growls out the question.

"Do about what?" Sloane asks with a frown.

"You can hardly go into the station and tell everyone that you got a hot tip from a psychic when you clearly don't believe in them," Logan tells him, and hears Catherine mutter, "I'm not a damned psychic," at his side.

Sloane actually looks dumbfounded – it appears he hasn't given that side of things much thought.

Throwing his hands up in the air, Sloane turns to Frank. "Any ideas?"

By the time Mrs Baines arrives at lunchtime, Logan and Catherine have gotten over the shock of discovering that she has a 'gift'.

"If I get anymore 'gifts' I'm going to start thinking my daddy was really Santa Claus," she tells Logan.

He actually laughs, his side-splitting rumble bringing Mrs Baines into the conservatory to see what all the fuss is about.

"Nice to see you both so happy," she grins, though it falters a bit when she sees Catherine scowl at Logan. "Did you enjoy your trip to Lakelands – I didn't get to hear about it last night."

Catherine's cheeks flame as she remembers that they had taken an impromptu early night.

"It was great," Logan answers when his guffaws die down. "Catherine's sisters and their husbands came down for an overnight stay, too."

"Well that sounds wonderful," Mrs Baines beams. "Did you find time to discuss the accommodations – I'll bet you were too busy with family," she adds quickly, not wanting them to think her forward.

"Oh, you are going to love it," Catherine pipes up, glad to have something else to talk about. "You'll have a suite of rooms all to yourself and then there's the nursery and our suite of rooms on the other side."

"Well, that sounds grand indeed!" Mrs Baines gasps in surprise. "I thought you meant I'd have a large double room – that would do to make myself comfortable in," she offers politely.

"The rooms are already there," Logan tells her. "And Caroline has offered to get them all fitted out and decorated – you'll need to collaborate with her to make sure your rooms are decorated how you would like them."

"I will," she beams, then turns back to her kitchen on a cloud of exciting possibilities.

"Should we tell her?" Catherine asks, and Logan knows to what she is referring. "After all, she may not want to live in a house with a 'freak'!"

"That's enough!" Logan's laughter is forgotten as his anger surfaces quick and sharp. "I don't want to hear that word in this house ever again! Do you understand me?!"

Although his anger is on her behalf, it still shocks Catherine to the core. "Ok. No need to get your Jekyll head on!"

Taking a deep, calming breath, Logan has to battle back his anger, it galls him to hear her disparage herself like that, and to think of all the others who have done so in years past.

"I'm sorry, but it cuts me to the quick to hear you talk like that!"

"Then I'm sorry too," and she reaches across the table to take his hand. "No more freaks in this house," she smiles, and he returns it ten-fold because he knows it's what she needs.

"I love you, Catherine. I love every part of you, and you need to start loving yourself!" He gives her hand a gentle squeeze then draws his back when Mrs Baines brings in a large plate of his favourite steak and onions with boiled potatoes and mixed veg.

The serving she puts in front of Catherine isn't much smaller than Logan's. "I made sure to give you plenty of steak and a little less potatoes," the housekeeper smiles indulgently at Catherine. "A bit of extra protein will do you and the boys nothing but good!"

"Thank you, Mrs B," she smiles happily now. "I just hope these boys won't grow as big as their dad while they're still inside me – think of the labour pains!"

At that, they all enjoy a good laugh and the tension is once again easy and light.

CHAPTER SIXTEEN

Later that afternoon, Catherine is working away on her computer trying to trace the monster back to his lair.

She has a connection to him – of that she is now certain. If she can just remember the part of her dream before he arrived at the house.

Allowing her mind to brood on that, she gets into the street cams, fast forwarding hours of film to see if she can spot anything familiar. When nothing clicks she sits back in her chair and tries to think things through logically.

I know he arrived at the house around two in the morning as that's when Logan woke me up. That means he must have been driving to it sometime before that – if I can find him on the traffic cams leading up to the house then maybe I can trace him backwards.

"Got you! Logan, I think I've found his van!"

Striding across the room, Logan looks at the still frame of a dark coloured van. "What makes you think this is his?"

"Because I traced it back from the Richerson's house and the time fits," and she points to the time shown at the bottom of the screen. "But if it isn't, I'm going to look like a complete idiot," she frowns at the screen, willing the windscreen to clear and show the driver at the wheel. "I'm not sure what to do with this – it's not like I can make out the number plate clearly."

"Tell them anyway," Logan advises. "What the police chose to do with the information is up to them, you can only give it to them!"

"Maybe I can find a clearer shot," Catherine muses, biting nervously on her bottom lip. "But I've already browsed through hours of film; this looked like the best of the bunch."

"Then go with it – come on, we'll call Frank and see what he says."

In the living room they sit waiting for Frank to get back to them. There had been no point in calling Sloane, he didn't believe in Catherine's dream anyway. Though how he explained to himself how right Catherine's information had been, Logan couldn't guess.

I don't want his negativity around Catherine – she can talk herself down without any help from Sloane, but he could make matters worse! And I won't allow that to happen!

The phone finally shrills into the nervous silence and makes Catherine jump.

Logan leaves her side on the settee and answers it. "Hello, Colson-Sayers residence," he speaks clearly into the receiver.

"Ah, Frank, did you find anything?"

Catherine is actually biting her nails till Logan frowns over at her and she realises what she's doing.

Standing, she joins him by the telephone and tries to hear what the inspector is saying. When she can't she simply pushes the speaker button on the keypad, then shrugs her shoulders when Logan looks down at her.

"My wife is now listening too," Logan tells the inspector. "Would you like to repeat that last bit?"

"I was just saying that we have managed to get a make and model from the picture you specified," the inspector repeats for Catherine's benefit. "Our lab boys are trying to get more on the number plate but have warned us not to hold our breath on that."

"I was wondering; I forgot to ask when you were last here but, where was Natalie when her parents were killed?" Catherine sucks in her bottom lip and can't be thankful that it was Fiona and Colin that were murdered instead of Natalie.

"Ah, yes, well," the inspector procrastinates obviously upset by the deaths. "Natalie and Joshua were getting edgy being locked up in their own homes, so to speak. So we arranged for Natalie to spend the night at Josh's house with his parent's permission, of course."

"Of course," Catherine repeats inanely. "I thought it might be something like that – will they let her stay on, in the circumstances?"

"Yes, they were most sympathetic and understanding when they found out about Natalie's parents. It's amazing how such horror can also bring out the very best in people."

"You're right, Inspector," Logan acknowledges. "I just hope you get him before any more people have to die!"

Replacing the receiver, Logan pulls Catherine into his arms and just holds her.

"I don't want you to go anywhere without me, ok?" he murmurs against Catherine's hair.

In his arms she feels safe and loved, "Why would I," she murmurs into his chest, and snuggles in closer. "I love you, too, Logan. With everything that I am, I love you."

The barbeque is blazing and the smell of grilling steaks fills the summer afternoon.

Henry is staying with Catherine and Logan for a couple of days and all of Catherine's family is enjoying the hot summer's day in the garden.

The happy chatter is constant, and Mrs Baines is enjoying a carefree day off cooking.

"Are you enjoying the wine?" Henry asks her, having topped up her glass.

"It's a rare treat – I usually buy the bargain bottles at Asda," she grins enjoying her indulgence, "but this is the real McCoy. I may not be used to quality but I know when I taste it."

Henry gives a whoop of laughter and Catherine and Logan smile at each other happily.

"Are you ever going to tell us what happened about that maniac you helped to find?" Caroline asks over the chatter which instantly stills to silence.

Logan looks at Catherine and gives an almost imperceptible shake of his head.

He's warning her not to spill the beans about her true involvement, judging this to be the wrong time for such an awkward revelation.

"I managed to track his vehicle," she tells them simply. "The police did it all from there."

Caroline doesn't look convinced and scoffs loudly, "They didn't have a clue until you got involved, what happened to suddenly fire up their little grey cells?"

"Catherine spent hours going over traffic cam footage once she knew the time of the murders of Natalie's parents," Logan tells the intrigued group. "The police acted on what she found so, in reality, their little grey cells didn't have all that much to do."

"So, do you know why he did it? Tom asks his daughter, and Catherine gives him a rueful smile.

Before she can answer, Caroline pipes up again. "He probably suffered some kind of abuse – a man doesn't just decide to start abducting and torturing people on a whim!"

"Actually, that happens more often than you might think," Mrs Baines tells them all. "Not all murderers are triggered by a traumatic event just as not all abusers were abused themselves."

"It appears to have been a mixture of all that," Logan observes quietly. "Niall Cross is the son of a GP. He trained to become a doctor – hence his access to medication and his ability to keep his victims alive after repeatedly beating and torturing them."

"A doctor!" Adrianne gasps in disbelief.

"I don't think we'll ever know the truth of it," Catherine tells them. "And I doubt we'll ever know, for sure, how many people he killed. I'm just glad he's locked up."

"How is Natalie doing?" Adrianne asks, full of concern for the poor girl.

"That's actually the best part of the story," Catherine smiles brightly for the first time. "Josh's parents have agreed to let her live with them – though it won't be for as long as they might have liked."

"Why?" Adrianne asks, enjoying Catherine's brightening mood.

"Natalie and Joshua are getting married," she announces, and a cheer goes up around her. "Natalie told me that what happened had shown them that life has to be lived in the moment, and they are going to live each day like it's their last, as it so very nearly was."

"Glad to hear it," Henry raises his wine glass. "To making each day count," he toasts, and everyone fervently repeats it.

"Did you get an invite?" Travis asks, thinking that Catherine and Logan deserved the thought.

Blushing, Catherine nods, "We did – though I told them they didn't have to do that. It's a family occasion, after all."

"But they might not be getting married at all if it weren't for you," Adrianne beams with pride up at her sister.

"I suppose," Catherine hedges awkwardly. "I just hope they enjoy their day; it's what Fiona and her husband would want."

"So what are you planning to wear?" Caroline asks cheerily.

"Christ! I don't know – have a look in my wardrobe and pick something out for me," Catherine suggests hopefully. "This maniac I married has stocked it to bursting!" And she gives Logan a dig in the ribs with her elbow.

"Not a chance!" Caroline tells her twin then looks over at Adrianne conspiratorially. "Time for some sister shopping – when is the wedding anyway?"

"No! No! No!" Catherine tries to protest, but when she looks from Caroline to Adrianne and back again, she knows all is lost. "It's a month away – by then I'll look like the side of a house so there's no point shelling out a load of money on a new dress!"

"Vanessa!" Adrianne pipes up victoriously. "She'll design you something amazing, and you know she can get it made in time – just look what she did for our weddings!"

With a hand clapped firmly to her forehead, Catherine tries to stay calm." Not the mad fairy – anything but that!"

Laughing along with her sister, Caroline fervently agrees with Adrianne, "You know she gets your style just right – look how often you wear that lemon creation of hers, and the other colour-ways you had her make it up in."

Closing her eyes in quiet acquiescence, Catherine finally nods her head, and hears both her sisters give a shrill laugh of excitement.

"When's good for you," she hears Caroline ask Adrianne.

"No time to waste, better make it tomorrow," Adrianne suggests eagerly.

Even the men are laughing at her plight, "Might as well give in gracefully," her father tells her when she finally opens her eyes to look at them all.

"Ganged up on by my own family," she shakes her head in disgust, but can't resist a small smile of appreciation.

They care about me. They honest to goodness care about me – the torture just has to be worth having sisters who care like that!

Vanessa Shelby, aka, the mad fairy, has a studio now. Her fame has spread since doing the wedding dresses for a famous pianist, a world renowned singer and the wife of a multi-millionaire.

"Aaaahhhh," Vanessa screams a welcome when all three girls walk in the door, and she begins boinging around like a mini dynamo.

Catherine pales, Caroline laughs and Adrianne gives the tiny woman a hug, once she stays still long enough to receive one.

"I got to work right after you called," Vanessa tells Caroline. "Come and look...come and see," she beckons with a forearm doing its best to imitate a windmill.

Catherine follows warily, eyeing the mad fairy as if she might do something crazy, which of course she does.

There are a couple of long tables laid out with fabric, and one of them even has drawers beneath it. But where does Vanessa decide to keep the sketches for Catherine – why, on the top of a nearby cabinet, of course.

Before any of the girls realise what she is about to do, Vanessa springs onto a stool, steps over onto one of the tables then up onto a shelf and reaches on top of the cabinet to retrieve her sketches.

With a triumphant, "Yeah," she leaps to the floor and comes face to face with a distraught Catherine who is holding her arms out as if to catch her.

"You damned maniac!" Catherine berates her. "Why the hell don't you use the drawers?!"

Standing stock still, the mad fairy's big green eyes blink up at Catherine. "They're safer up there," and Vanessa shoots out a little arm to point to the top of the cabinet.

Caroline and Adrianne are laughing, shaking their heads at Catherine as if she should have known better.

"Come on, Vanessa, let's have a look at your masterpieces," Caroline urges.

She has drawn six different designs and three views of each.

Even Catherine can see what a brilliant artist she is. "You could frame these and sell them," she tells Vanessa, forgiving and forgetting her antics of before.

Beaming a smile that causes her green eyes to glint jewel-like, Vanessa is thrilled that the girls really like her sketches.

Catherine frowns and Vanessa looks suddenly worried.

"You don't like the designs?" she squeaks anxiously.

"No. I mean yes," Catherine gives a shake of her confused head. "It's just that I had an idea is all."

Looking and blinking her round eyes, Vanessa's head of short multi-coloured spiky hair tilts to one side voicing a silent question.

"I don't suppose you still have the sketches you did of my wedding dress, do you?" she asks awkwardly.

Catherine could almost see a bulb ping on above Vanessa's head when her eyes blink even wider and a tiny finger goes up in a 'aha' motion.

When she moves, Catherine is ready to head her off from the cabinet, only to find that Vanessa has gone in the opposite direction.

There are at least half a dozen boxes, almost as big as the designer, standing to the side of the door they had entered through. Bending over one of them, Vanessa all but disappears into it.

When she emerges, her smile is triumphant as she holds aloft the searched for sketch.

Rolling it out for Catherine to see, Vanessa is touched by her reaction. "I felt beautiful in this," Catherine states without a hint of vanity, her fingers trailing the outline of her wedding dress. "And Logan loved it."

Vanessa slides it from the table and re-rolls it gently then lays it across both hands and holds them out to Catherine. "For you," is all she says.

With watery eyes, Catherine takes the gift and has to firm her lips together to stop them from trembling. After swallowing down hard on the tears that are threatening to fall, Catherine simply says, "Thank you. Thank you so much."

From then on, Catherine and the mad fairy become good friends with a new understanding between them.

Although Vanessa still keeps her most precious working sketches in the highest, safest places, she makes sure to get them down before Catherine arrives.

EPILOGUE

The wedding day arrives and the sun shines bright and beautiful in the clear blue sky.

Although Natalie no longer lives in the house where she was raised, and where her parents were murdered, she is getting married at the same church where her parents got married in Upper Stanton.

The villagers have worked hard on the church grounds to make them especially beautiful for their bride.

Garlands of flowers are strung in swags looped over y shaped stakes in the ground to form an outdoor aisle leading up to the open church doors.

Two large wrought iron standards, with flower arrangements atop them, are stationed on either side of the entrance.

Everything about the church says welcome. Everything the villagers have done says, we're sorry for your loss and we are thinking about you on your special day.

When Catherine and Logan arrive, they are greeted by Joshua who personally escorts them inside to their seats.

The church is as beautifully decorated as the grounds outside. And once again, the villagers are responsible and collectively bore the cost.

Catherine is amazed by it all – that strangers could take this couple so much to their hearts is beyond anything she has known in her life. But it is no more than she would like to have done herself.

Her work, at Fiona's behest, may have saved Natalie and Joshua's lives, but it hadn't saved the woman herself, and that was a great weight on Catherine's heart.

Stood on an easel at the foot of the vicar's podium, Catherine sees a large photograph of Fiona and Colin Richerson on their own wedding day in that same church.

Natalie's parents may not be in attendance in the flesh, but their spirits are already present, of that Catherine is absolutely sure.

When the church bells begin to chime Logan takes Catherine's hand and gives her a broad smile. Then the organ sounds and the church comes alive with music.

The groom and his best man move to the front of the church and everyone is on full alert for the change of music...and then it happens, the wedding march begins and every heart present swells with love.

Love of their wives or husbands, love of their mischievous children, but most of all love for this couple starting out on the greatest journey life has to offer.

Walking down the aisle on her proud uncle's arm, Natalie is beautiful, as all brides are on their wedding day. But the beauty is not in the dress she is wearing, or the bouquet of lilies that she is carrying – it is in her eyes, and in her smile, which tells the world how very much in love she is.

The monster has been defeated. The wedding is testament to that. But it makes Catherine think, and gives her an off-the-wall idea.

"I want to start a detective agency," she tells a stunned Logan when they arrive back home. "I want to help people like Natalie and Joshua, like all those other people that monster harmed – I really want to kill the bastard," she states forgetting herself. "But as I can't do that, I'll set my brain to catching his like and putting them behind bars!"

"You amaze me," Logan tells her, staring at her with such wonder and pride in his eyes. "I don't even know why I'm surprised by your idea – I should have seen it coming...but I didn't."

Lifting a large gentle hand to cup her cheek, Logan dips his head to place his lips softly against Catherine's. "My psychic warrior!" he chuckles quietly.

"I'm not a damned psychic," she protests stubbornly, but isn't really annoyed at the reference to her dream.

"If you really want this, I'm all for it," Logan says, and surprises a smile from Catherine. "I'll even help when I can."

"You are! You will!" she gasps, then laughs at her own incoherence. "I'd better sharpen the brain-pan if I'm going to be any good at it. Now I just have to figure out how to tell Ben!"

"Oh, I don't know," Logan narrows his eyes but his smile still lingers, "he'd still do anything for you. If you asked him to continue the business single handed he would – but the fact is, he has David and Emma to replace you."

"Err, that is where the problem lies," Catherine ignores Logan's innuendo and concentrates on the real problem. "I want Emma to work with me. She's good and she's quick and I happen to like her."

"Well, that's high praise indeed coming from the computer queen herself," Logan laughs, then frowns at the tricky prospect. "You are not only planning to leave most, if not all, the work to Ben but are actually going to poach one of his staff to start up your own agency." His frown deepens, "And when are you planning to tell him this delightful news?"

"Tomorrow, first thing," Catherine bites her bottom lip nervously. "You know, you could come with me – just moral support," she tells him when he raises a brow.

"There is nothing I would like better, but sadly I can't." Logan frowns; he would have enjoyed seeing Ben's shocked face when he got the news. He never has been able to forgive him for wanting Catherine, even if the better man had won the fair maiden! "Damn it! There's no way I can get out of my meeting – I've already put it off once."

"Never mind, I'll see to it – I don't think he'll mind what I have to offer him."

As it happens, that was a complete understatement. Ben is thrilled!

"You really want to do this – you haven't hit your head or had some kind of brain-storm – you really want to 'gift' me the business then go off and start your own detective agency?"

"I do," Catherine frowns at Ben's obvious delight to be running the business without any interference from her.

"Now if you can stop sounding so damned pleased about me leaving, I'll tell you the rest!"

"What? It can't be anything better than what you've already told me," Ben states with an ear to ear grin plastered all over his face.

"I'm taking Emma with me – I've already asked her, and she's all for it, so don't argue," Catherine warns him, but is surprised by his reply.

"Great! Fine! Just don't ask David to go too – I draw the line there!" he tells her, his manic grin not slipping in the slightest.

When she gets back home, Catherine tells Logan about her conversation with Ben and his unexpected attitude.

"You'd never think he'd declared undying love for me less than a year ago," she frowns over at Logan as they sit in the conservatory enjoying the colourful gardens.

"You just told the man you are giving him a multi-million pound business – what did you expect, tears?" Logan asks, incredulous at his wife's unbridled generosity.

"It's just money – you're not mad at me are you?"

Shaking his head, Logan lifts an arm and drapes it over Catherine's shoulders, "I probably should be, but no. It was your money to do with as you please, if giving Ben the business makes you happy, then so am I." *And I get him out of my hair. A good deal, all in all!*

"Good! I spoke to Henry about Emma's living quarters and he said the lodge was almost habitable," and she grins up at her husband with open adoration. "This is going to work - a new start for us, and a new business to sink my teeth into."

Then her smile turns grim, "Monsters everywhere beware, Catherine Colson-Sayers is on your case – from now on, there will be nowhere to hide that I won't find you!"

*****

If you have enjoyed reading this book, please leave a review at the place of purchase, thank you.

Susan Elle